Murder the Light

THE DEMON WHISPERER #2

ASH KRAFTON

Red
Fist
Fiction

Art and design by Red Fist Fiction

First edition published 2017

Contact Information can be found at **www.ashkrafton.com**

**Murder the Light (The Demon Whisperer #2)
by Ash Krafton**

Hell hath no fury like a woman scorned...especially the woman who'd been scorned by the King of Hell himself.

Chiara's been abducted by her own mother: an Enochian defector who's taken up arms against the Light. Simon makes the ultimate deal with her father to get her back...but he'll have the Devil to pay.

ISBN: 1-946120-07-3
ISBN-13: 978-1-946120-07-6

Murder The Light:
The Demon Whisperer
Book Two

ASH KRAFTON

DEDICATION

To my beloveds:
my husband, my children, my family

CONTENTS

CHAPTER 1.. 1

CHAPTER 2.. 7

CHAPTER 3.. 13

CHAPTER 4.. 16

CHAPTER 5.. 22

CHAPTER 6.. 25

CHAPTER 7.. 33

CHAPTER 8.. 40

CHAPTER 9.. 48

CHAPTER 10... 59

CHAPTER 11... 62

CHAPTER 12... 69

CHAPTER 13... 77

CHAPTER 14... 83

CHAPTER 15... 88

CHAPTER 16... 91

CHAPTER 17... 95

CHAPTER 18... 102

CHAPTER 19... 108

CHAPTER 20.. 111

CHAPTER 21.. 121

CHAPTER 22.. 131

CHAPTER 23.. 136

CHAPTER 24.. 139

CHAPTER 25.. 143

CHAPTER 26.. 148

CHAPTER 27.. 160

CHAPTER 28.. 166

CHAPTER 29.. 169

CHAPTER 30.. 172

CHAPTER 31.. 178

CHAPTER 32.. 185

CHAPTER 33.. 193

CHAPTER 34.. 198

CHAPTER 35.. 202

CHAPTER 36.. 206

ABOUT THE AUTHOR............................ 217

Charlestown
Boston, Massachusetts

Heavy bass notes thumped through the cinder block wall of the dingy men's room. A single working halogen light glared overhead, casting suspicious shadows under the walls of the stall.

And it reeked in here. Honestly. No reason you couldn't keep a restroom clean, even if it was in the basement of a junkie club. Wasn't there some kind of law?

Simon Alliant wiped off the toilet seat and carefully sat down. Not that he actually worried about catching a funky STD through his jeans, or anything. He wasn't in here to do the usual business.

And he had absolutely no intention of being caught with his pants down tonight.

Sounds of retching came from the stall next to him, the splats of someone who didn't even try for the toilet. Probably an actual junkie. Better to sit on the can and puke on the floor than be fooled into thinking heroin would let a guy stand up and take proper aim.

The smell hit a moment later. He cupped a hand over his mouth and nose. Wing sauce. Yech.

With his free hand, Simon fished around in his pocket, feeling for the charm he wanted. A tube of metal, half a finger-length long, a few degrees cooler than anything else. Ah. That's it. He pulled it out, the thin light glinting off the surface of the silver whistle.

He put it to his lips and gently blew. No sound. None a mortal could hear, at least. That didn't mean it didn't work.

A blue wind stirred in the space between him and the locked door, hovering over his knees. Blue wind. Never found a better way to describe the phenomenon. Technically, it was a mass of winged air elementals, so great in number that they churned the air enough to flutter his hair back. The reflection of the ceiling light bounced off their minute wings, illuminating the iridescent membranes with a cerulean haze. So, yeah. Blue wind. They'd swarm for a few minutes before wandering off, drawn to another elemental summoner (or quality dog whistle). It's what they did.

They also created enough of a breeze to sweep out the offending odors of the hot mess next door. Simon inhaled deeply and grinned, appreciating the respite. Practical magic was the best magic.

No longer distracted by the druggie in the next stall, Simon rolled up his sleeve. Gingerly, he fingered the edge of the tattoo on the bend of his arm and sucked a breath between his clenched teeth. Still sore from the last hit. The ink made it hard to tell if the skin was red or bruised but, did it really matter? It felt like it had been scalded, the quintessential sunburn.

The sensation made him hesitate. It wasn't just magic. Wasn't just charms and chants and wicked cool light shows.

This shit did physical things to him, left a mark. It was one thing to cut a thumb when a little blood was needed, but this kind of magic was different. It came from within and hurt him on its way out. One of these days he might just blow a hole in his arm.

The thought was almost enough to make him put the wand away.

Almost.

He popped off the cap with his thumb before stowing it. Wasn't like the wand was sharp, or full of ink or anything. The cap was simply to keep the end clean. Exorcism was dirty work. The last thing he needed was to get ectoplasm or demon goo on it. Who knew what would happen if a splash of evil got on the live end of a wand? Or if he tried to use it afterward?

Genuine shudders ran down his neck, tumbling between his shoulders. It would be like sharing a needle with every addict in Hell. Not a chance he wanted to take.

The music swelled as the door swung open and someone staggered in, making a lot of noise for a simple trip to the urinal. He sighed. The environment wouldn't improve any time soon. And this was long overdue. He'd been putting it off and putting it off. Couldn't put it off any more, not if he wanted to think straight tonight.

His mind wandered back over the past few weeks. He had managed to distract himself with a new charm he'd picked up near Philadelphia. The spell required to prime it was written entirely in German and those umlauts were a real pain for a Boston mouth to get out. He'd had to practice the pronunciations for four days before he was brave enough to attempt the actual chant. The charm itself was loads of fun, though, and well worth both the effort and the six hours he spent in the police station explaining his way out of a ridiculously simple misunderstanding.

But the distraction couldn't last forever. Eventually, the signs started creeping in. Muscle aches he couldn't explain. Anxiety over losing his magical edge. That damn yawning—

And an itch in his brain that he couldn't scratch because it wasn't physical. That part was completely mental. A sign that he wasn't keeping his core happy. His magical core. The place where magic made complete sense, where it sparked and swelled and flooded his system. When his core went unjuiced, he felt the repercussions all over, on every level, in every one of his senses.

He rubbed his hand over his eyes, picky and dry and tired. Just a little wand hit. He didn't have to go overboard. Just one little tap. An itty bitty buzz. He didn't need more than that. Just enough to take the edge off so he could think straight again and get that damn job done.

He gripped the wand between his thumb and index finger as if weighing a dart. Exhaling through pursed lips, he positioned the wand over the center of the tattoo. Lowered it. Slowly. If he lined it up just right, he'd hit the metaphysical center of the rune and more or less mainline it. Wouldn't need more than a touch to give him what he needed. Didn't even need to supercharge the tattoo with the chant beforehand. This was just a sip.

Slowly.

Contact. His breath leaked out in a low groan as the wand pressed against his flesh. That sunburn. The touch of wood on flesh was otherwise unremarkable for just the briefest moment.

Then the rune recognized the contact for what it really was.

A fiery light zipped around the outer edge, bright enough for retina burn, before the entire tattoo pulsed with a sullen throb of light.

And then it *lit him up*—

Simon's head snapped back. Eyes wide, irises ghosted grey, pupils like pinpricks. The magic flash-fired through him, scalding him, soothing him, seducing him, sating him. Pain and pleasure, pins and needles everywhere. Like swimming in sex made of broken glass. The universe exploded behind his eyes and he saw it all, could smell it, taste it—

And then it was gone.

The restroom returned. He was on his knees, face smooshed up against the cold metal of the stall door. Hand clutched around the wand so tight his nails bit into his palms. Taste of blood in his mouth.

The magic had completely faded but not before he'd caught a glimpse of what he needed to see. He replayed every detail over and over, trying to hold onto the visuals, and struggled to memorize the vision before it slipped away like an opium dream.

Wiping his mouth with the back of his hand, he saw the rusty smear of blood. He must have bit his tongue when he hit the door. And he could taste what could only be described as toilet stall door. Jesus. Found the one flavor nobody would ever try to sell for vape juice. His lucky day.

Thank God this was a bar. At least he could sterilize his mouth with a shot or two.

He pushed himself upright and spit into the toilet before flushing it with his foot. The sudden change in position was too much. His head swam, his legs wobbled, his vision going a little white around the edges until his blood caught up with him.

He secured his wand under his wristwatch band. The tat was quiet, his insides buzzing pleasantly, his core happy again. With both hands, he patted down his pockets, taking a quick inventory. Okay. Deep breath...

Big mistake. He gagged, the acrid odor made him choke. Not like a janitor had been in to mop the floor while he'd been wand hit tripping.

He shouldered open the door and shuffled to the filthy sink, running the water. Ice cold. Mmm. He ran his hands under the stream before rubbing his face, his hair. The cold gave him some real contact with the world, a sense of crisp cleanliness.

Just a ruse. Inside, he was as filthy as the floor upon which he'd been kneeling.

Should have bothered him that he had little regret. Why bother with regret when he knew he would do it all over again, as soon as the craving became too much to ignore?

He stared at himself in the mirror, dark eyes made darker by the bruises beneath them, the lousy light overhead. Looked like a death mask.

One day, he'd wear a real one. But not today.

Today, he had a job to do. A life to save. This bottom-feeding was only a pit-stop.

Chiara. He had to find her. And thanks to this little something-something, he not only had a clear head—he had another clue. A face to find. A face that would lead him to her.

With that tiny fragment of vision still burning in his mind, he plugged a cigarette into his mouth and strode out of the restroom, renewed and refueled.

And revolted, still. He'd have to chew this cigarette if he wanted to get the taste out of his mouth. He made a straight line for the bar. Double vodka. Anything less would fail to banish that evil on his tongue.

Simon clambered up the last steps of the fire escape and swung his legs over the low cement wall rimming the roof of the bar. From here, he could see just about all the neighborhood, the lights of Boston Harbor off in the distance, the last signs of life before the blackness of the lightless sea.

Traffic sounds were muted and innocuous. Even sounds of people coming and going on the streets below him were gentled. Laughter, shouts of greeting. The distance and the steady breeze from the water washed out all the hard edges. From up here, it was easy for a guy to be fooled into thinking there was peace on earth.

Not this guy.

Simon sucked down the last of his smoke, grinding the butt beneath his foot. Holding his scrying lens up to his left eye, he peered down over the edge at the people milling around below. Nothing. Further off, the streets nearby. Still nothing. Scanning in an ever-widening sweep, he scrutinized every window, every street, every sidewalk.

Show me that glow. Tell me he's out there. That face he saw in his wand hit-induced vision. He had to be close. A face that Irish had no business being anywhere but Boston.

"Nothing, Simon." A mellow voice sounded from behind him, carried easily through the light wind. "This city is quiet tonight. You'll not find anyone to fight this evening."

"I will, if I look hard enough." Turning, he saw Mack standing a few yards behind him, looking as enigmatic as ever. Then again, he was an angel. "Always someone worth fighting."

"Yes, if you include yourself in the mix. Why do you continue doing this to yourself?"

Simon scowled. "You make it sound like I'm abusing myself."

Lifting an eyebrow, Mack tilted his head, flicking his gaze to Simon's arm. "Are you not?"

"No." Simon crossed his arms. "I'm not. Look, Mack, I know you don't get the whole 'humans and their base needs' thing but this isn't abuse."

"What do you call it?"

"Sustenance," he said firmly, as if he believed it. "A necessity. It keeps me going."

"Like your nicotine?"

"Yep." Simon tugged his pack out of his inside pocket and lifted it in a salute to the angel. "Just like it. This is me. This is my baseline. If I don't keep the baseline stable, I can't function. And I need to function."

He hunched and ducked to block the wind, cupping his hand around the lighter as he lit his smoke. Drawing deep, he relished the scrape of smoke in his throat, the quick buzz in his limbs, the blueish plume he exhaled into the wind. Three cheers for oral fixations. "And I need you to function, too, bro. News?"

"Not since last week's Ladder," Mack said. "There has been no new development."

"And even that wasn't a ton of help. You played a re-run. What good is that?"

The angel looked affronted. "A prophesy from the Metatron is no less important simply by being repeated. If anything, it reinforces the importance of the message."

Simon groaned. Wasn't like the prophesy had been very useful the first time around. "Okay. So. *Light's scion, tarnished...Love's betrayer...A crushing blow will deliver to the lone-heart, the mortal savior of souls.* Nothing new at all? Not even like maybe a point in the right direction?"

"Point? To where would we point? The answer is inside you."

"Uck. It's really not." Simon sighed, stowing the lens. "If it was, she'd be home."

"Perhaps you waste valuable time looking for that woman."

Simon eyed him. "Weren't you the one who wanted me to think that prophesy was all about her in the first place?"

Mack shifted his gaze away, over the neutral cityscape.

"Uh, huh. Right." Simon nodded with aggravated vigor. "So if the Metatron is still yelling about her, then she must be important."

"Simon—"

"No, sir. You can't back-pedal, Mack. And you can't be biased, either. I know you don't like her. But just remember one thing—the reason you don't like her is a reason that comes from no fault of hers."

"I cannot like or dislike anyone. Personal preference is an expression of freewill."

"But you do, by trying to herd me in the direction you interpret as the correct direction." Simon inhaled deeply on his cigarette, exhaling a long cloud that streaked away on the breeze. "I'm not some moron apprentice with no experience. She's better than you give her credit for."

He walked to the edge and crouched down, lipping his cigarette. Turning his head, he spoke over his shoulder. "She saved my ass, Mack. It's only fair that I save hers."

The angel leaned to put a hand on his shoulder. "Maybe she is not in need of saving."

Simon huffed a laugh, a hard sound of disbelief. Standing, he chucked the smoldering butt over the side. "Well, maybe I still am, and she's the only one who can do it. Either way. I'm going to find her." Turning, he folded his arms. "And I need you. You still in?"

"I cannot fathom why I should not be."

"Good. Because I got a clue. A face. I don't know who it is, but they know something. That face is the person who stands between me and her."

"All right." Mack folded his hands below his abdomen. "Tell me about this face."

"Eh." Simon scratched his head. "That's the tricky part. I didn't exactly—see it. For real. It was a vision."

"A vision?" For an angel, Mack did *doubt* surprisingly well.

"Yeah." He couldn't sound anything other than sheepish. "You know. A vision."

The angel shrugged, dismissing the notion. "You do not have visions, Simon."

"I do." Christ, it was hard to not feel five years old when Mack used that tone. Sometimes he pushed the whole *child of God* thing a little too far. Then again, who knew just how old Mack was? Did angels have birthdays? "Sometimes. Magically-induced visions."

"Your…tattoo?" Mack sniffed. "A drug-induced hallucination."

"No. This was actually a thing. I'm not creative enough to make this shit up."

Clearly having had enough of human shortcomings, Mack took a deep breath. His eyes flashed gold as he invoked the power of his influence. "Explain."

Simon felt the angelic touch on his psyche. How did a guy explain it? The vision was a flash flood of omnipotence. In that moment he'd seen all, heard all, known all. A human brain couldn't hold on to all that, no matter how sustained that moment might be. But that one image, that one face, had jumped out of the flood like a breeching whale, huge and important. Nothing else mattered except that one sudden appearance.

The face was just a face. Not remarkable enough to describe, other than he'd recognize it when he saw it. It was what came with the face.

A sensation of flight, yet darkness.

Things of the dark didn't fly. They were chained to the bottom of all bottoms.

Could be another dual-divinity, like Chiara. But it didn't feel like Chiara. It felt—out of place. Just odd.

Yeah, he knew she was one of a kind, but still. If that face was of the same ilk as she, something should have resonated.

Right?

Shit, he didn't know. A glance up at Mack's drawn brows made him think that the angel wouldn't know, either.

And, considering who that angel worked for, the guy could be pretty darn judgmental sometimes.

"The face was unremarkable. Just some dude. But there was a major feeling of…" Simon eyed Mack, carefully selecting his words. "Conflict. Spiritual conflict. Like clashing polarities."

"So. Human? Or Divinity?"

"Looked human. Then again, most of the time, you do, too. Except when you…" Simon waved his palms, like jazz hands, at the sides of his face. "You know. Do the thing."

"Yes." Mack smirked, shrugging his shoulders. The fog of his ghostly wings billowed behind him. "The 'thing'. Well. The 'thing' makes me think that there is nothing new to find here, Simon. You've doused in every town between Belmont and the Atlantic. She is not here. You would have found her by now."

Simon's stomach went to rocks, suddenly heavy. He hadn't wanted to admit it. But Mack was right. He'd actually resorted to dousing, mage pre-school level, just trying to catch a wisp of her. She wasn't here.

"Perhaps it is time to go back to Baltimore," Mack said.

"You are more comfortable there. Here, you are not."

"But I grew up here. This is home." Odd word for a feeling he couldn't remember. Maybe if he said it enough...

"Not anymore. You closed all your doors here, Simon. Leave this place. Baltimore gave you shelter and you feel like you are in your own skin when you are there. And she was there, at least once. Perhaps you will pick up a trail there."

Simon eyed him, searching for some sign of deception. Mack didn't approve of Chiara but he was too much an angel to lie. Out of all the people on the planet, Mack was the only one he could trust. And he wasn't even people.

"Maybe you're right," he conceded. "You want to take us there?"

"I most certainly can do that." Mack nodded. "The usual landing?"

"You mean, at the diner? Yeah. Need to make sure the van's OK."

"Alright. Come." Mack wrapped his arms around Simon from behind.

As the fog of angel wings surrounded Simon a desperate thought flashed into his brain. "Wait a sec, maybe it's too soon to travel. I was just in the bar—"

Too late. Mack opened the portal and hurtled them both through time-space-existence. The rush grabbed him by the belly and spun him head over heels into infinity. He only had the frame of mind to clutch onto two thoughts. One was that prophesy. *Light's scion, tarnished...*

The other thought was the certainty of a very, very rough landing.

Marietta District
Atlanta, Georgia

The view from the corner office was nearly panoramic. This high up, there was little to obstruct the view. Minimal framing interrupted the wall to wall, floor to ceiling windows. No glare, no reflections. Just 270 degrees of visibility that spread the city out like a beach blanket.

During the day, the city sparkled like crushed diamonds, sunlight glinting off chrome and glass and the shiny pieces of mortality scattered about the streets far, far below. The rising heat of summer streets made the air waver, giving motion to the light and creating the illusion of sunlight upon a dancing ocean.

At night, the cityscape and the starry skies melded into one, making her kingdom appear deep and dark and boundless.

It was rather like standing on a mountain, with all the world spread out before her. Minus the annoying wind and most likely filthy trudge to the top. She didn't look this good by accident, after all.

Luminea stood in the corner, inches from the glass, hands hovering near the panes. Glass. Cold, hard. Brittle. Breakable. Glass was made from little more than heated sand. With a simple gesture, she could blast it all the way back to its humble origins.

But, no. She wouldn't. It takes an ordeal for a handful of dirty sand to be transformed into pristine, perfect glass, so pure that one had to touch it to be sure it was even there. Nearly invisible, deceptively strong, and utterly capable of sealing off the world.

She respected glass. She understood it.

Right now, she stood in a tiny box, encased in glass, encapsulated away from the rest of the world. One day, her perspective would reign. It would not be she in the box. It would be the world, and the world would lay upon the palm of her hand. And she would grind it back into sand.

She closed her eyes and inhaled through her nose, flexing her fingers, unknotting the fists she'd unwittingly made. Such emotions were for the deep, not for the surface.

A rap at the door broke her introspection.

"Come," she said.

The door opened behind her. "She is awake, madam."

She needn't look to see who'd spoken. Even if she didn't recognize the voice, she knew there was only one person who had the authority or the clearance to be here. She only needed one person.

"Thank you, Zophiel." She turned to look at him, mouth down-turning when she saw his face. She clucked her tongue. "Really? A ginger?"

He bowed low, eyes to the ground. "A temporary inconvenience, madam. I was rushed."

"Mmm. See to it that it is very temporary." She turned back to the cityscape, where twilight was rising in the distance, blanketing the ocean in misty shadow. "Oh, and Zophiel?"

"Yes, madam?"

"See that my daughter is ready to receive me. I will be down directly."

"Yes, madam." The door closed behind her.

Luminea pressed her palms to the glass. Hard, rigid glass.

So much like that which had once been a heart.

Baltimore
Maryland

Simon stood in the parking lot across the street from the diner he called home. Well, *home* was a loose term. More like *home base*.

His head was still swimming with the after effects of the portal. God, he loved those things. Zipping through time and space in an eyeblink that felt like a pinprick of infinity, a peaceful, restful, no demons chewing on your ass kind of happy place. It was the only place he never felt haunted, or chased, or damned.

Portals were how angels traveled. Holy wormholes. They all had VIP passes for the pearly gates, too. Simon's trips with Mack through them, the goody-goodness he experienced there, made him dare to hope maybe once all this horseshit on Earth was done, his soul would end up someplace bright.

He'd be pleased even if he ended up somewhere in the neighborhood of the light. Heaven's suburbs. That would be swell enough for him, considering his time alive was being spent in the demon-infested ghettoes of an exorcist's vocation.

He rubbed his eyes and stretched out a hand to steady himself. Still a little woozy. Small price to pay for first class travel and a taste of the Great Beyond. Mack hovered like a nervous aunt, looking like he worried Simon would face-plant the bumper of the Toyota he'd propped himself up against.

They'd arrived to find the van perfectly unmolested. The chicory really did its job this time. Invisibility spells weren't hard to pull off and they were super-effective but the longevity was sporadic. Sometimes they didn't last as long as a guy wanted.

Like when a guy had to leave town and stayed away longer than he'd planned because his partner got abducted.

Mack had stuck around only long enough to make sure Simon wouldn't pass out in the parking lot and get run over in the darkness. Said *angel business called*. A Ladder, a Summons, whatever. Simon didn't know.

Didn't care, either, because at the time all he'd been able to think about was whether or not that last vodka would stay down. Despite the thrill and serenity he always felt during a portal, physics was still physics and alcohol was no remedy to avoid motion sickness.

A cup of coffee or three in the diner and he just might be good for the night. Considering how long he'd been away, tonight would be a long one.

He staggered across the street, taking a moment outside the diner door to pull himself together. Not too crowded tonight, a handful of regulars he recognized to varying degrees. Kelly was behind the counter, late shift again. Her mom must be staying overnight, watching the kids. Loud music playing from the kitchen. Rainier on the grill, then, and Shug on the register. Shug was hard of hearing so he never minded the radio. Who knew if he even heard it?

He waved to calls of "Murph!" as he sank into a back booth. Out of the way, quiet, near the can. In the corner. He could see everyone, everything. The waitress came over with a mug and a full pot, pouring him a hot cup before setting it down. She made a little chatter: work, kids, how'd he been, looked a little rough, better leave this here and save her multiple trips across the dining room.

He endured her care and thanked her. Coffee, quiet, and a safe place to rest before heading out to work.

He'd missed Baltimore. The sounds, the scent of the air, the people. Boston had its northern charm, to be sure, but none like Charm City. He'd learned and forgotten the lore behind the city's nickname once he'd made substantial inroads in the battle against the rising dark. His charms were the only ones he cared about.

But there was something else about Baltimore he'd missed. Chiara. What they'd started here. What they'd faced. She'd sat at this very booth with him, right there across from where he sat now, pretending to eat a fruit cup.

He laughed and rubbed his mouth to cover it. The look of surprise on her face when she'd bitten into that first piece of cantaloupe. What a kid—

Sobering, he pulled the carafe toward him and poured another cup. Wide awake. Widely aware of what was wrong with Baltimore. With Chiara missing, it lacked a certain hope.

In his eyes, anyway. Most days, his eyes were the only ones he looked through. It made him biased.

He sat for another thirty minutes or so, fueling his caffeine machine and planning out his night. He'd been away for weeks so there was no telling what he'd find out there. Pulling a twenty from his front pocket, he smoothed the bill and left it on the table. Extravagant for a couple of coffees, but he knew how hard Kelly worked to raise her kids. With any luck, they'd stay in the Light she worked so hard to guide them toward.

May as well start at the front sidewalk. He walked a quick salt circle around the building to reassure himself that at least this place would remain his safe house before striking off to find the closest ley line. Ley lines were streams of power that flowed beneath the surface of the earth, like an invisible underground river system. Old cultures recognized magic, its influence upon the visible world.

Today, only a handful were trained to detect the flow of mystical energy beneath their feet. Far fewer than the hoards that found it by instinct, fed from its power, and used it to manifest things not meant to walk upon the earth.

Dropping deep into his subconscious, he walked, feeling the strength of the ley lines, seeking the larger streams, following them and watching keenly, on the lookout for abnormal activity.

He spent most of the dark hours dousing and measuring pendulum swings, keeping notes in a mini-notebook, the kind grade school kids used to write down their homework assignments.

The flat pencil he kept with it needed sharpening. The tip had been worn down to the point where it needed more attention than simply peeling back the wood to renew the lead. Around five in the morning, he'd taken out his pocketknife to freshen its edge, but when he cut his thumb, he knew he had it throw it all in. Wouldn't want to accidentally blood a pencil. Who knew what kind of fresh hell a nine-year-old could cause with it if he dropped it in the street?

Was as good a time to quit as any, besides. All the ley lines were just as they'd been when he left, and there were no major breakouts of Dark activity. Quiet here, too. He'd covered more ground than he had anticipated, thanks to the wand hit and three large coffees.

Once he'd gotten his physical bearings, he realized he was too far from his neighborhood to walk back to the van. Worse yet, he didn't have enough chicory to hitch a ride with an unwitting driver. Daylight was too far off to go hunting along the roads for a fresh supply. When he tripped over his own feet, he knew it was time to call it a night.

Time to bunk it in the boonies. Hip, hip, whatever.

He found a motor inn that didn't ask why he didn't have a motor and took the cheapest room they had. Which, by the way, was any of them.

No one remarked that he didn't have more than the clothes on his back, either, but that's just good customer service. Don't ask, don't tell, don't pay attention. It all suited him fine.

He'd once briefly considered getting a backpack for these walkabouts, just so he'd look like he had more purpose to be walking about. But really, besides his amulet, his wand, and the charms stuffed into his pockets, he had little else.

And, as he lay on the lopsided bed after a surprisingly decent shower, he realized he didn't really need anything else.

The humidity was raunchy, but even he wasn't brave enough to prop the door open. The AC was crap and the ceiling fan only a little better. Simon stared up at its slow rotation, the odd slanted shadows it threw onto the ceiling, and rubbed his chest, his fingers running over the edge of his amulet.

His constant companion. He'd only taken it off when Chiara went down that staircase in Belmont.

He chuffed out a dry laugh. The staircase in Belmont. What a mouthful. Still, it was easier than saying Hell.

And the time before that, the last time he'd been without his amulet...he breathed heavily, a sudden weight on his chest. The anxiety was real. Memories seemed so much more immediate when it was dark.

Kent. The last time he took his amulet off was with Professor Kent.

Kent was old school. English magic—now, there was a true example of tradition. The old gent was a pillar of tradition with his tweed jackets and the way he never went without his cap. He was disciplined, well-spoken, as resolute as the Tower of London, and quietly, masterfully, powerful.

In short, Kent was everything Simon was not.

Curiosity had drawn Simon to Kent, but that wasn't what kept him. Simon was green, his magical education spotty and eclectic. Kent was the Holy Grail of mages.

Absolutely mind-blowing. There wasn't a topic Simon could toss up that Kent didn't spike over the net. Not a single trivia question he couldn't turn into a demonstration or lecture. Not a single random musing that Kent didn't turn inside out and hand back to him as if he'd solved a Rubik's cube in under fifteen seconds.

Simon knew apprenticing would not be easy, and would most likely be painful. But he never thought that, at the end of it all, Kent wouldn't give him back his amulet. Instead, then prof disappeared, taking Simon's stamped-circle of soul with him.

Kent seemed like he'd have been classier than that.

He hadn't even released him. Just up and left in that decisive enough for today way he had, only he didn't come back the next day, or the next week, or ever. Simon spent the next three years nearly out of his mind while he hunted it down and got it back.

Shit like that left a mark on a man's soul.

And it wasn't the thirty months of near-insanity because the metaphorical key to one's your psyche/soul/magic/everything was just out there, somewhere, who knows who had it or what they'd do with it—

It was the abandonment of all he'd come to think of Kent. The reverence, the respect. He hadn't given it easily and having to revoke it wounded him, terribly.

He tugged the chain out of his shirt and rubbed the amulet between his thumb and forefinger. He had it now. That's what mattered. Pressing it to his lips, he swore a promise to it and to himself. Never will that happen again. Never will he feel like that again.

Never.

Marietta District
Atlanta, Georgia

Chiara paced the perimeter of the unfamiliar suite a sixth time without discovering anything new. Three rooms. Bedroom, parlor, and bathroom, all sumptuously decorated. High-end furnishings, an antiquated style she'd admit she found aesthetically pleasing, if she'd been asked.

But she hadn't been asked. She'd been dragged here by the force of Enochian magic, against her will, by a woman who never did anything without making a complete spectacle. If it was worth doing, Mother would often say, it was worth watching.

Without a pause, Chiara started circuit number seven, fairly certain she'd seen everything she would be permitted to see. It didn't stop her from looking.

It was what she didn't find that drew her brows together in a furious line, agitation snapping her footsteps with every renewed circuit. Not a single clue to reveal where she actually was, nor the faintest memory of how she got here.

She frowned deeper. Not a door, nor a window that could be opened, not even a mysterious sliding panel. No ways in. No ways out.

And she was wearing herself out trying to find one.

The rooms were bathed in a soft beige glow that seeped in from the walls and ceiling. Not noticeable at first, when she was pre-occupied with finding a route by which to escape. It was only after she'd begun feeling along the walls, knocking, listening for a pocket door, that she discovered the light source was the confines of the room itself.

And it wasn't through odd technology. The light was a byproduct of magic. Enochian magic. Specifically, wards that hampered her power. At least, the paternal side of it. Somehow, she didn't think it was a base-model feature. This room had been built specifically for her.

This room had been Hell-proofed. She felt it in every bone. The deprivation felt very much as if her ears had been completely stopped up and she could only hear her voice from within her skull. It was uncomfortable and disconcerting and made her worry her defenses were compromised.

After no less than a dozen passes, she dragged a chair into the barest corner where she hoped no one could sneak up on her and drew up her feet, hugging her knees, waiting. Worrying.

The last thing she remembered was sitting in his car, watching him go into the store for a new pack of cigarettes. Then her mother's face beside her own, an arm around her neck, a yank that made her feel like she left a piece of her soul back in the car—

Then nothing. A brief light, then blackness, then she woke up on the bed in the other room. No indication of time, or place, or what would happen next. All she could do is sit, and stare across the room at the full-length oval mirror that stood in the corner opposite. She sat and watched the reflection of herself huddled in the spindly-legged chair, eyes wide and worried, looking very much like a war orphan.

But that wasn't for whom she was most worried.

What happened to Simon? Was he okay? Was he here somewhere, looking for a way out, thumbing through each of the charms on that key ring of his, discarding each failed attempt before launching a new plan? He would be hard at work, looking for a solution. A man of action, he was.

But that didn't comfort her as much as she wanted. She knew he had a tendency to get…emotional about his decisions, when he wasn't acting on pure impulse. Simon would get a solution, one way or another, and wait for the bill to arrive later.

Normally, it would land him in his usual type of trouble. This was completely new territory. He didn't know who was behind all this.

And she didn't know if he was here in a similar prison, or back at her home, or even alive.

She hugged her knees a little tighter and rocked. Which would be the worst of the three?

So, she waited. Waited for something to change, and wondered what she'd say to her mother when the wait was over.

Simon spent three days working in the same particular fashion, days, nights, everything in between. Mapping, scouting, chanting, dousing. When he'd finally made his way back to the city center, he destroyed the dousing rods and scattered the pieces. Either they were broken, or he was.

Nothing. Not as much as a blip. It was like the whole world had finally gone light side up. And he felt utterly defeated about it.

Lighting a cigarette, he leaned against the front window of a coffee shop, swirling the dredges of a coffee regular. He lipped the cup, one last taste of the now-cold coffee before he chucked it into the barrel. This was just a city. A quietly boisterous city that stood up to evils far worse than demonic possession.

Still, there was one place he hadn't scouted. One street uptown. One house in particular.

Hers.

Somehow, he'd managed to circumvent it on each of his rounds. Maybe that was the problem. He hadn't been ready to face her house. If she wasn't there, he'd have to admit that she was really gone.

He sucked hard on his cig, spitting out a lungful of smoke. He'd gotten pretty good at facing shit these last few weeks. How hard could looking at a building possibly be?

Deep down, he expected to find nothing more than a beat rat-trap three decker, empty to the rafters. Her suite had travelled wherever she'd went. If she wasn't here, it wouldn't be here, right?

He'd started walking without realizing it. Maybe it's what he should have done in the first place. Litmus test, right? If her suite wasn't there, neither was she. It would have eliminated half a week of demonic detective work.

He was almost there when he got a lump in his throat and a pain in his chest and he suddenly couldn't hear the street noise over the racket of his heartbeat. Chiara's place was around the corner and four doors up. And then, the wondering would be over. All questions would be answered.

He needed to know. He just didn't want to.

The row house looked no different than the ones off to either side, other than the general disrepair. Not decrepit, *per se*, just not quite as unabandoned. No curtains fluttered in open windows, no flower boxes or folding chairs on the stoop. He could see a discoloration above the door, pieces of old board. Once, a weathered sign that read ROOMS TO RENT had hung there. As he climbed the last step, he saw the broken remnants of it laying in front of the door and tried not to think about it. He shouldered the sticky door open and slipped inside.

Everything was the same. The leaves and old pizza shop flyers, yellowed and brittle in the corners. The dim, oily lights. The smell of stagnant musty disuse. But it was quiet. Quiet, still, and empty. He felt it in his gut.

Up the steps.

The door stood slightly ajar at the end of the upper floor.

For a moment, his plan seemed to crumple up like a used paper towel. That gap in the doorway made the apartment look less than occupied. Would it hold nothing but littered floors and yellow stained walls, cracked windows and graffiti?

He wiped his nose and shook his head. Made it this far. Might as well have a look see and put it to bed, once and for all.

He slid down the wall toward the apartment and place his palm of the door. Holding his breath he pushed it in, hard enough to bang it against the inside wall. It made a vacant, hollow sound. He grimaced and tapped his mouth, hesitating.

What the hell, he thought. He could stand out here and wonder, or he could step in—

Something grabbed him by the front of his shirt and yanked him around the corner into the room. The door slammed shut on the empty hallway.

He shook himself free of the invisible grip, swinging blindly at the empty air. Nobody. Nothing. Nothing he could see, at least, in the dimly lit room. The only light came from cloudy windows, streaking down through a thin haze of dust motes.

He straightened his shirt, deflated. Just as he feared. Ugly, old, empty apartment.

Or was it?

With the door shut behind him, things began to slowly change. The fireplace roared awake, hungrily devouring the logs within. Color seeped out of the fireplace like molten lava as the firelight flashed across the floor, stretching up to the high ceilings. The palatial apartment came alive, renewed, as the fire grew.

He looked down at his shirt where he'd been grabbed. A faint glimmer of opalescent sparkles faded like an evaporating stain. They were the same hues of Chiara's chrism.

Her magic. Her wards.

The wards had known he was outside and drew him in, yanking him the last few steps when he'd hesitated. Thinking hard, he realized he'd felt a tiny drain on his energy, like a moment of weak knees. The wards didn't want to disable him.

The apartment needed him. It needed him to exist.

Which was probably a bad sign. Why would it need him if Chiara was all right?

He stooped to light a cigarette at the fireplace. By now, the apartment had reached full glamour, looking every bit like he remembered. It pained him to see her junky couch, looking more abandoned than ever.

He needed to find her. Just so that her junky couch could be appreciated by someone. What a terrible existence, to live alone after losing the only person that cared.

"Stupid couch." He dragged deep on his cig and stared at the dilapidated sofa. "So. What do I do now?"

The couch said nothing. Which was a good thing. Last thing he needed now was possessed furniture.

Lipping his smoke, he sat down on the couch, feeling it creak beneath him. "If I were her, where would I go to look? Where is my strength? She stayed down here, right? Didn't like to roam the place. Bit of a grudge against her dad. But he's powerful big stuff, yeah?"

Not like she'd ever dropped more than a hint. She didn't like to talk about her divine heritages. Chiara preferred her mortality to the infinite power of her mixed blood.

He puffed out a smoke ring, watching it waver, musing. "But it wasn't her dad that hauled her off, was it? It was someone bright. And if there's anyone who'd be willing to help me get her back…"

He glanced up the staircase, pondering the upstairs floor with its impossibly long hallway, its collection of eclectic and luxuriously hedonistic rooms. By his measure, anyhow; any bedroom with an actual bed had to be designed for sin, even if only the sin of laziness. He didn't much consider beds for sleeping. There were more like sporting goods.

But the room at the end of the hall…*that* room didn't have a bed. And when she had been in danger of bleeding out from a should-have-been mortal wound, that was exactly where she'd wanted to go.

The creepy pool.

He was on his feet and halfway up the stairs before he was aware he'd gotten up from the couch. His hand was on the doorknob to that last door before he even had a plan.

And what little plan he threw together last minute was a pitiful weak one.

The sulfuric smell assaulted him the minute he stepped inside. No point in holding his nose. The odor overwhelming, creeping into his pores and smothering him from the inside out.

Monstrous iron braziers burned with sullen glows in the corners of the grey-lit room, the ceiling hung up in shadows too deep to pierce. And yet, a light hung sullenly over the center of the room, reflected by the odd silver sheen of the pool's surface.

He shuddered, remembering that pool. He'd watched Chiara shove herself in and sink beneath the surface. He'd sat for a chunk of forever, watching the still water, not knowing if she was ever going to come out.

Glancing around him at the stone floor, he pulled a salt bag out of his pocket and scratched the back of his head. This was as good a place as any. If he was going to get the attention of Chiara's father, might as well do it from the room that felt most like a vortex of dark energy. Honestly, if he were deaf and blind he'd swear he stood in the center of a tornado, the power pulling at him like a vacuum and the pressure making his ears hurt. And his tattoo—

That tingled beneath his sleeve like there was a glob of minty pain liniment slathered on the bend of his arm. Never a good thing when the tat was sore before he'd even had a chance to use it.

Time to get this circle up before other things started to hurt.

He compass-drew his salt circle, using the two-foot length of jewelry chain he kept for his pendulum. Last thing he wanted was to take a chance. A wobbly border could weaken the protective circle. And considering what kind of power he was about to go calling upon—

Maybe a second ring of salt wouldn't be such a bad idea.

Standing up straight, he ground his shoes against the stone tile, wanting as solid a connection to the earth below him. Another slight problem if one mentioned that technically this floor didn't exist but, meh. No time for quibbling.

After a brief debate, he proceeded with a classic Alpine circle chant. The Alps were pretty much all stone and water. *And beer*, he thought in a flash of irreverence. Well, the celebratory drinks could come after he got Chiara home. This room was nothing if not stone and water. And fire. But that last part was definitely not the image he wanted for this circle.

"*Stein und Wasser.*" He summoned his deepest mental magic and sank into the rhythm of the German verses. "*Hören Sie auf meine Stimme. An meiner Seite stehen. Mich vor Schaden zu schützen.*"

Stone and water. Listen to my voice. Stand by my side. Protect me from harm.

He bit his tongue, hard enough to taste blood. Carefully, he dropped a thin stream of pink-tinged saliva onto his right index finger.

"All righty-roo," he said. "Raise the circle, old boy."

Leaning, he curled his thumb and flicked his fingers at the salt ring.

When the droplets of blood hit, the salt took up an eerie luminescence, a pale green glow that rippled along the thick white line until the head met the tail. When the circle completed, a pulse ran around like a neon heartbeat. A good, solid connection. This circle would hold even in a windstorm. He would be safe in here.

Now, to ring the demon's doorbell and to try not to run.

He closed his eyes and counted his breaths. *Ten, nine, eight—*

Hard to focus on a summons when a guy wasn't sure exactly who he was trying to call. All he could do is meditate on Chiara, who she was, what her dark side felt like. He'd gotten to know it well when they'd first met; she'd done this little peek-a-boo into his brain that left a sooty stain on his mental workings for a few days afterward.

She hadn't meant to hurt him. It was just what it was. She didn't flaunt her divinity, not either brand. Still, it was a little disturbing just how comfortable she was with using that power when she needed it.

So. Chiara's face. Her power's feel. Somewhere dark. Over and over he repeated simple chant, sinking deeper into a meditative trance, sending out a beacon. *Six, five—*

Hear me. Talk to me. For her.

Three.

Two.

One.

He pushed out a breath and opened all his senses, physical and metaphysical, drinking in the energy around him. It rose, like water in a glass. Building. Something was coming.

Something big.

Something way too fricken big. He cracked his eyes.

Water had seeped out over the edge of the pool, toward him. *Don't get wet,* she'd said. Warily, he eyed the silver stream as it oozed toward him, like sentient mercury. When it reached the salt, it bounced back slightly, as if repelled.

He leaked out a breath of relief.

The metallic liquid circled around, testing the salt circle even few inches. Each time it touched the line, it recoiled briefly and slid along. Like it possessed an intelligence.

When it had travelled all the way around, it joined in a gooey blob of coherence, a moat around his fortress.

"Ok," he said. "You know I'm here. I know you're here. Just crawl back into your pool and we'll get along famously."

The liquid swelled a little, like a button mushroom, looking at him.

"Go on." He waved his fingers at it. "Shoo."

The button-blob sank back into the thin stream of mercury.

He smiled, self-satisfied.

Suddenly, the ring of silver water grew, stretched up in a cylindrical sheet, forming a tube around him. No spell could stop it. He knew nothing about that water, its nature, its properties, its alignment. All he knew was he had better not touch it.

But the water slowly rose around him. Higher, up to his knees, his waist. He couldn't jump it if he had to. As long as his circle held, as long as he stayed inside—

Then it occurred to him. He'd never explored the complete dimensions of a salt circle. Was it more than a two-dimensional thing? How high would its protection reach around him?

The metallic sheet rose higher, eddying and swirling against his invisible fortress. Up to his chest. His neck. Over his head.

He watched the silver walls stretch taller and taller. Would he be trapped? Would the air run out?

When the water curled overhead and came crashing down on him, filling his so-called protective space, scalding him with a freezing heat he couldn't comprehend, he didn't have time to ask the really important question.

Could he survive?

All he could do was scream. Scream and let the blackness take him.

Chiara had dropped into a light trance, the stillness and the constant soft light dimming her wary alertness.

Motion and a soft, hollow ringing sound from the other side of the room caught her notice, jarring her into action. She snapped forward, scanning, straining every sense. The surface of the mirror shimmered and fractured the light, its glinting catching Chiara's attention.

Glass didn't move that way. Chiara chewed her lip. The mirror wasn't made of glass, then.

The ripples rolled wider and wider until they filled the frame of the long mirror. A moment later, the surface split. A figure emerged.

She was tall, easily six feet in height, and every inch was graceful, lithe. She stepped through the mirror as if she stepped off a curb and paused, hand on her hip, angling her body to provide a good look.

Her blazer was an expensive cut, tapered at the waist, wider at the shoulders, reminiscent of the 90s executive look. Long, slim legs beneath a knee length pencil skirt, ending in stilettoed pumps. An iron-grey power suit, paired with vicious heels. The wardrobe was engineered to be intimidating.

Golden hair was swept back and coiled into an elegant roll, leaving a short angle of smooth fringe. There was nothing to distract from the porcelain beauty of her face: the icy blue eyes that held no heat, the red-lipsticked smile that carried no warmth.

Beautiful, severe, completely in control of all she considered to be hers. Chiara included.

"Darling," the woman said, spreading her hands in a prim parody of welcome. "So glad to see you've settled in."

Chiara uncurled herself and stood, not remembering if her mother had outgrown her longtime preference for curtseys. Well, it was the twenty-first century. There would be no curtseying here. "You could have just called, Mother."

"Would you have answered?" Luminea sighed. "Mothers and daughters never get along. Everyone knows that. That's why we have sons, to heal the wounds our daughters leave."

"Sons—" Chiara cocked her head and stared intently at her mother. Just how much had she missed out on during their time apart? "Do I have brothers?"

Luminea huffed out a scornful sound and brushed her lapel. "I have no sons. You were my first and, as it turned out, my only. I just—I don't know, imagine sons are easier than all this."

"Talking is easier." That was something they rarely did, if at all. Hard to converse with someone when viewpoints were so dramatically skewed. And, anyway, it looked like there wasn't going to much of anything except talk, not with those wards. "Let's begin with you telling me why you brought me here, and when you will allow me to leave."

"Really, as if I can keep you here." Luminea pouted a moment before abandoning the feint. "Oh, wait, I can. You have come up against the wards, I imagine. Too curious for your own good. It's better if you stay here in your suite. Other places are…less hospitable."

"There are other prisons less hospitable?"

"If I had you in a prison, you would know it." Luminea cleared her throat and visibly relaxed herself with a shrug of her shoulders. "I wanted us to have a chance to catch up. I know how much you prefer your independence. I needed a way to persuade you to stay."

Chiara tried to assume an impassive expression. Very difficult for a person who didn't bother to disguise her feelings around mortals, not even Simon. But Luminea was different. She was a keen observer, as well as an opportunist. Best to not give her anything she could use against her later on. "What is wrong? Something has changed again. I can tell."

"Nothing has changed, darling. But that's the problem. And we are going to fix it."

"Why do I feel so suspicious?"

"You are your father's daughter. Trust never came easily to you."

There, finally, was an element of heat: the scornful emotion that carried out upon the word *father*. Her parents had never gotten along.

A mild statement. The animosity her mother demonstrated toward him was quite astronomical. All her earliest adult life, Chiara had been forced to use a unique type of diplomacy when dealing with the issue. Avoiding the issue generally proved to be an impossibility. Quite frankly, it became much easier to avoid her mother altogether.

Chiara sighed. It was once again time to reassume the diplomat's role. "I am your daughter, too."

"Yes, exactly. That is why you are going to be the remedy to all this."

"All—what?"

"Simply everything." Luminea sat down on the armchair, perching on the edge of the cushion without settling in.

"Chiaroscuro, when you were born, I wanted you to be everything I could not. I am of the Light. I spent my existence in the Light. In Enochia. Surrounded by friends, my family. Our faith."

"I know," Chiara said, her voice gentled. "I remember the stories you told me. But you never told me one thing. Why did you leave?"

"Ah. That was not a tale for bright-eyed children. But you are no longer that child." She got up and paced slowly to the window. "I wandered. We Enochians are allowed to sojourn, you know. To see each Plane, each level of God's Creation. Oh, the wonders…"

Her voice fell to a breathy murmur. "Oh, I shall never forget my wandering. Such worlds, such amazements. The Sphere of Infinite Space—such incomparable bliss! I wished never to leave…"

She turned slightly, wagging a finger in warning. "But bliss, you see, is a barrier to true enlightenment. We cannot learn if we are entirely content. We cannot experience. And so I left bliss behind, because it was the responsible thing to do. And that was when I met your father."

That heat crept into her voice again, now paired with a gravity that felt like a change in air pressure before a storm. Luminea shrugged off her blazer and draped it over the back of chair. "And I wasn't allowed to return home. Not after He…touched me."

Silently, Luminea slipped off the shoulder of her dress, baring her skin, and half-turned. "This is what happens when Lucifer turns you from the Light."

A black hand print stained the skin of her left shoulder.

"Oh, Mother." Chiara was aghast. Mother had never shown her this mark before. Why had she kept it secret?

She went to her mother's side to inspect the mark. With gentle fingers, she brushed the slightly-raised edges. Ragged and cracked, like a burn. A brand. She'd been marked. "How have you kept this from me?"

36

"All I did was turn toward Him. His voice. His words. He was so...alluring. I didn't even know that I had turned away from the Light. All I did was..." Luminea pulled away and tugged her dress back into place. "No matter. This place was here. Open. Neutral. And we did well here on Earth, didn't we? You had an enjoyable childhood, didn't you?"

"Of course, I did, Mother." Chiara reached for her mother's hand, wanting to provide some modicum of comfort. All this time, Luminea had been hiding a bottomless shame. What an awful way to live. How many sacrifices had she made to provide her child with a happy life? "I know it wasn't easy for you. It's hard to raise a child on your own. Even today, with all its modern conveniences. I cannot fathom how mothers do it."

"Well, those times are over, for me. You're not a child anymore. You have no need for a mother's care, do you? You are self-reliant." Luminea smiled, a cloaked version of pleasantry. "Well. Sort of."

"What do you mean?"

Luminea spread her hands. "Do you see all of this? This apartment, this fortress, this empire? I built this. I am self-sufficient. I relied on no one. But you—still living in that quaint little glamour your father keeps for you, no?"

Chiara looked away. "That has nothing to do with you."

"You are absolutely right. So perhaps I am feeling a bit passed over these days. You take benefits—monumental benefits—from your father but you don't even spare a thought for me. The one who raised you. The one who gave everything up for you."

"You didn't give it up for me, Mother." Sometimes diplomacy was too difficult a farce to maintain, especially when the attacks became pointed. "You lost it because of him. Don't blame the child for the actions of the parents."

Luminea clucked her tongue, giving her a shrewd smile of admiration. "Oh, I don't blame you, darling. You were the only good thing that came out of it all. But...I think that I have suffered long enough. Centuries of feeling scorned—by my lover, by my child. I need to put the past firmly behind me. I may no longer be capable of another sojourn to the Sphere of Infinite Space, but I understand there are entire philosophies in this world dedicated to freeing a soul of such burdens, allowing me to heal and move on."

Was her mother capable of enlightenment? For her sake, and for her mother's, she ardently wished it possible. "I truly hope so."

"Abandon useless ideas like hope, darling." Luminea smiled, once more as icy as her eyes. "It's a brutal thing."

"Well." Chiara rubbed her hands together. "Are we finished? I'd like to go home now."

Luminea stood and donned her blazer, fastening the buttons. "I'm afraid that's not possible."

"This grows tedious, Mother."

"Only because you make it so." Luminea smoothed her hands down her willow thin body, the satin lapel overlay making her look stiletto-sleek. Her voice made a velvet sheath for the blade of her body.

"No, you make it so. By keeping me here. Against my will."

"Will." She sniffed an amused sound. "Free will, do you mean? I didn't think you possessed it."

"Of course, I do, Mother. Just as you do."

"None of us are free, Chiaroscuro. None. We are all a slave to something."

"I can't believe you even let those words come out of your mouth. You've never been a slave to anything."

"Oh, but that is where you are wrong. We all have our demons."

Chiara looked away. "Sorry if I cramped your style. I know single mom was never the role you imagined for yourself."

"You are not my demon, Chiara." Luminea strode over to her, taking her fiercely by the shoulders. An unusual light glinted in her eyes, a thawing of the icy fortress within. "You are my daughter. The best thing that ever happened to me. I don't regret one single moment of you."

Chiara stood in her mother's grip, feeling more like a child then she'd ever felt in her life. The show of maternal vehemence was such a rare thing, a jewel to be treasured. If only there wasn't such dark subtext. "Then why do I get the feeling that I'm about to pay for something?"

"Nonsense." Luminea rubbed her arms briefly before letting her go. "You are my guest. I think you'll find your suite most comfortable. If there is anything you require, just ask."

With a perfunctory smile, she tipped her head and strode back to the mirror. Audience adjourned.

Chiara called out after her. "How about a door?"

"I'm sorry?" Luminea paused and turned around.

"A door, Mother." Chiara crossed her arms, thoroughly tired of the emotional games. This conversation had been as informational and as frustrating as she'd assumed it would be. "A door that lets me leave."

The woman laughed, a false, pretty sound. "Why would you want to do that?"

"I have a life to lead."

"No, you don't. Not anymore." Clearing her throat, Lumina switched voices. "Lunch will be up shortly. Poached salmon. You'll love the sauce."

She smiled, no sign of the telltale fin, no cut of the surface. Chiara knew better than to think the waters were safe.

Luminea peered into the mirror and smoothed the edge of her angled bangs. It needed no grooming. She was picture perfect. Always had been. She lifted a finger and pressed it to the center of the mirror. The surface shimmered a moment, rippling, before it reached toward her, pulling her in.

Gone.

All that and she was none the wiser. Chiara frowned, acutely reminded of countless past conversations that had ended the same way. The last one had been the one that drove her out into the world, away from her family.

So typical of her mother.

Simon snapped awake, lying downstairs on the tiles in front of the fireplace. The fire was blazing, flooding him with an uncomfortable heat. He scooted away, letting the cooler air wash over him and soak into his damp clothes.

Dammit. He failed.

Well, okay, just half a dammit. He was alive, after all. His last sight had been that of a waterfall of molten silver crashing down on him, his last sensation that of mind-bending pain. He felt his arms, chest, legs. Amulet in place under his shirt. Everything seemed in order.

But he hadn't been able to make contact with Chiara's father. So, dammit. He failed.

Maybe another trip up to the pool was in order. Had Chiara installed some safety mechanism to protect him? Did the apartment itself protect him? So many questions. Only one way to answer them, and that was to go back upstairs and try again.

He turned toward the staircase. Something odd in the stream of his periphery made him stop cold, colder than the room.

First of all, the room was different. Lamps of every style imaginable lined the room. Chandeliers hung from the ceiling. Groups of candles burned in masses scattered upon the floor, the wax melting together in puddles. Everywhere, the illumination of contrived light, none of which had been there when he'd gone upstairs earlier.

But there had been something else. With a muffled groan, he paused, really not wanting to look and confirm his suspicion. Really *really* not wanting and feeling quite possibly slightly alarmed. Fear solidified like an icy puddle in his lower belly, making him swallow hard.

He tilted his shoulder and swung a look toward Chiara's couch. His breath was blue fog in the frigid room.

Wasn't a couch anymore. It was a chair.

Rather, it was a throne.

Suddenly, failure wouldn't have been such a terrible thing by comparison.

Simon stood in the center of the strange room, knowing that he'd really stepped in something. Maybe this wasn't such a good idea.

"Well, you still have your wits about you." The unfamiliar voice was cultured, oily, and deeply masculine. "That's got to be counted in your favor."

Simon counted to three before summoning the courage to look.

A man in a suit stood at the top of the stairs. Simon knew it wasn't the butler. This man had his own atmosphere and it was the darkest kind of dark he'd ever encountered. It wasn't just dark; it was refined and…breath-stopping.

Bad, bad, bad. Simon liked power but he had no business admiring that stuff.

The man smiled, laughing softly, and descended the stairs one slow step at a time. "You can't help it. And it would be rude to withhold compliments from one's host."

"I know you," Simon said, his blood pooling in his feet. "I don't know how. I have never seen your face or heard your voice but..." His voice cracked and splintered into a whisper. "God help me. I know you."

"He won't, you know." The man stalked toward him, his dark eyes hypnotic, his gaze gripping. "Help you. Trust me. I know."

"Why does it feel like every ounce of blood in my veins is drawn to you? Like you're a magnet to the iron in each cell—"

"It's not chemistry, mage. And, don't worry. It's not lust, either. I know you're particularly concerned about that. Sorry. You're just not my type. But this—" He simulated a back-and-forth motion with his hands. "It's because you live on magic. Stolen magic. Stolen power. Power that belongs to me."

Belonged to *him*? Simon had done a bit of spell thievery in the past, sure. Not all knowledge was passed from master to apprentice. Sometimes, a book is read that ought not to be read. Sometimes a charm is liberated from its owner. But Simon never took something without knowing whose it was. That was plain old honor amongst thieves.

He stared at the stranger's aura, sifted through the man's darkness as if he stirred bathwater, trying to pin a name down. "You're not a demon. My amulet would be going nuts if you were. A mage? No. None I've ever met. I don't forget a face."

"You are correct, sir. I'm no mage. But I am what every mage secretly desires to become. The all-powerful. The mighty. The unconquerable. Second only to the selfish Creator himself."

A cold sweat bloomed on Simon's face, trickling down his neck, between his shoulders.

"Of course, you know me," the stranger continued. "Because I own you."

The man shrugged as if correcting himself. "Or, to be technical, I will. Eventually. No one lives forever."

Simon's mouth went cotton try. He tried to swallow and gagged. "Lu—"

"Shh." The man lay a slender finger over Simon's mouth. "Think before you say it out loud."

Think? If he'd been thinking, he wouldn't be here right now. So much for that. "Chiara's father. You're..."

"Lucifer, at no one's service." The Devil swept a sardonic bow. "Sorry if I deflated the drama you tried building. I have no patience for it."

"No worries," Simon said, his voice faint.

Lucifer smiled, a wide show of gleaming teeth, and pointed at him. "I know *your* name, Simon Alliant. And I did not invite you here."

Simon wanted to back pedal and run, just run screaming. His feet were rooted like thousand-year-old pines and he swayed in horror. In thrall. It was hard not to be.

The Morning Star. The First of the Fallen. The Enemy of God. The Satan. He'd been called so many names and had done enough to deserve each and every one of them, countless times over. But that wasn't what Simon saw.

No, there were no leather wings, no red pointy tail or wicked pitchfork. There was only a tall, trim man, with wide shoulders who knew how to cut a suit and just how to wear it. Hair, coal black and perfectly cut, sideburns trimmed yet long enough to hint at a touch of rogue—every detail was handsome, masculine, stylish, attractive. Even to a guy who definitely preferred women.

It wasn't His appearance, or the deep timbre of His voice, or the command in His dark eyes. It was power.

This man was the most powerful creature on this side of the Heavenly trench and God help him, please, because he knew it. He felt it. He resonated with it.

Here stood before him the pillar of evil, the ultimate sinner, the symbol of everything Simon stood against—and all he could do is sway on his feet, transfixed in Lucifer's gaze, hanging on every word.

He was a fricken goner.

"I've had my eye on you," Lucifer said, conversational-like.

It ran a tremor of terror through Simon's veins, a zing of adrenaline that made his hands and feet buzz. "Not a good thing," he choked out.

"Agreed. It's best to avoid my notice. But you have trouble with that, do you not? You like to be noticed."

Simon gulped and palmed his amulet, which lay cool and still beneath his fingers. His greatest protection was behaving like an ordinary trinket. "I'm not here to gawk or..."

"Remind me why I do not like you?" Lucifer tilted His head and lifted His brows.

Oh, shit. There was a condemnation if ever one existed. "Definitely not that. I'm here for Chiara. She needs help and I need yours. Oh, shit. I can't believe I said that."

"If she needs help, she'll ask. Or she'll take." The Devil pressed His lips together into a thin line, looking very put out. "She's had no qualms about doing it in the past."

Holy crap. Of all things he'd imagined the Devil to be, Disgruntled Parent was not on the list. "Not if she's in bigger trouble than she can handle."

Lucifer flashed an irritated look at Simon. "If she were in trouble, I would know it."

"Then where is she?" Came out too much like a demand. Won't get anywhere bossing the Boss around, not on his home turf. He swallowed thickly and humbled his voice. A surprisingly easy thing to do. "Please. I can't find her."

Lucifer turned to the fire, stretching out His hand. He turned His head, His profile drawn in severe lines. "I...cannot see her."

"Shit." Simon interlaced his fingers and held the back of his head. "If you can't see her..."

"It does not mean she is in trouble. If she is in a place of the Light, I cannot pervade with my sight."

"Is the Light always a good place to be?"

"Oh, that would be a matter of some debate." Lucifer's tone was decidedly amused. "Tell me why it should concern you."

"Because she didn't just walk off into the Light in search of puppies and unicorns. She got grabbed. Kidnapped."

"Kidnapped?" He scoffed. "As if she were weak enough. By whom?"

"I don't know. It happened so fast. She was sitting in the car and some lady appeared inside with here, grabbed her around the neck, and *poof!* They both just disappeared. No wake, no trace, no clue."

"A woman?"

"Blonde hair."

"And?" Lucifer narrowed His eyes.

"That's all I saw. I was in a store and saw it happen through a window. I couldn't see details."

"You saw them. You are simply too mortal to be able to recount them. May I?"

Lucifer shot out a hand and grabbed Simon's wrist.

The room went black at the edges and he felt like he was falling forward amidst a sea of voices. Just as quickly as it started, it ceased, shutting off with a snap.

Lucifer's voice was a liquid growl. "Luminea."

"Lumin-who?" Simon shook his head, trying to dispel the dizzy shadows that swirled through his sight. If Chiara left a residue, the Devil left an oil slick.

"Her mother." Lucifer exhaled through his nose. "That is why I cannot see her."

"Really? Her mom? So, then she's okay? And I popped in unannounced at what I'm guessing is tremendous mortal peril for no good reason?"

"I didn't say that." Lucifer jerked His head as if they commiserated over beers, complaining about their old ladies. "Her mother is...complicated."

"As in..." Simon rolled his wrist, prompting him to explain.

"As in you have no place in this, Alliant. You have spent a lifetime playing with tiny powers you don't even understand. Do not hope to understand this."

His condescending tone ground against Simon's sense of

self-preservation, loosening the hold he'd been keeping on his smart-ass mouth. "Listen, pal. I might be a puny human, but I had parents. I understand what *complicated* means. I'm sure my dad said that about my mom more than once and I still understood her."

Lucifer spun and leaned into him, full-on, making him back up a step. "Then understand this. If Luminea has her, then you may assume her intentions are less than maternal."

"Fantastic."

"And you have my attention." Lucifer withdrew, putting space between them. "You can expect my intervention in this matter."

"Does that mean you'll help?"

The Devil arched a brow, distaste in every line of His expression. "Hell does not help."

"Oh." Didn't know quite what to say to that. Other than cheek. "So, this is Hell, eh? Not so bad. Always figured there'd be a smell."

"There would be a smell," Lucifer said, a smile creeping up on the corners of His mouth. "If you were actually breathing. But you're not."

"Excuse me?"

"You're lying in the bottom of a pool. Dying." Lucifer turned His back on Simon, gazing at the fire again. "Maybe you need to run along."

Simon remembered, too late. The pool. The creepy pool.

"Son of a—" Simon raced for the stairs.

"Actually, no. I'm not." The amusement in Lucifer's voice was unmistakable. "I'm only my Father's son."

The Devil's laughter chased Simon as he took the stairs two at a time, not sparing a single glance back.

Would the pool be in the same location here? If it wasn't, he was screwed.

Lucifer called out when he reached the top of the staircase. "By the way, you owe me one."

Simon paused, his chest starting to burn. "Why?"

"Because I did you a favor. You'll see."

Ah, Hell. Literally.

Simon dashed down the hall, trying not to peer into the open doors. The sounds coming out of them were absolutely the stuff of future nightmares.

The pool. He had to get to the pool.

But the door at the end of the hall never got any closer, no matter how hard he ran. The hall kept stretching longer and longer like an eighties horror movie. Desperately, he reached into his pocket, fumbling for his keyring of charms, and chanted a desperate plea—

And hit the door to the pool room with his shoulder, crashing open the door with a bruising impact that took the last of his wind.

The pool. Not the same. Chiara's pool was silver. This one was…hazel green? The color of Chiara's eyes.

Eyes were the portals to the soul. Simon staggered to the edge and dropped in, sinking like a brick. Submerged in a sea of gold and green, he fought his way to the surface, every cell in his body on fire.

He broke the silver surface, feeling the scald. Sputtering, lungs screaming, he dragged himself up onto the ledge and rolled. More like…flopped a few times. His limp arm slid to the stone tile, fingers landing on the remains of his blooded salt circle.

His ragged gasps echoed off the stone. Took a whole lot of them until he was brave enough to look back over to the pool.

The waters were still. No one had followed him.

He grabbed a pinch of salt and threw it over his shoulder with a weary laugh.

Blurry-eyed and muffle-headed, Simon lurched down the hall, missing the first step on the staircase and sliding ungracefully to the parlor. He was almost glad she wasn't there to witness it. Not one of his coolest moments.

The greasy sheen of shadow on everything he looked at— he expected that. The Devil had just taken a look-see into his brain, just like Chiara had when they first met. If the kid had left a shadow, the Devil would leave a complete blot of impenetrable of darkness.

It faded, though. By the time he'd stumbled out the door, his sight had more or less cleared and he was able to do a mental inventory of his parts.

Still in one piece. A relief, that.

Down on the street, Simon reached into his breast pocket for his smokes, more out of habit, needing the comforting caress of the cellophane-wrapped pack. Something was off.

Something he couldn't put his finger on.

Never mind he'd just portaled to Hell and back. That should be enough to shake a man's moral convictions. But, no. In hind sight, the feat was a bit diminished on the apocalyptic scale. After all he'd seen, all he'd done, it had been just a new corner to turn.

If anything, he was surprised he'd even been allowed to leave. Was a real by-the-skin-of-his-teeth kind of moment.

He flicked open the box and lipped out a cigarette. Had to be something he missed. Every word, every nuance. He'd been over it a million times before he'd even gotten out the front door.

You owe me one.

I did you a favor.

Those weren't things one wanted to hear from the mouth of the Devil Himself.

Reaching for his lighter, he palmed it, turning it over in his hand. Maybe Lucifer had already done something to help Chiara. He'd been concerned about His daughter. Her disappearance had been a surprise, and an unwelcome one at that.

It was only a slip, a flash, but Simon had seen it. He'd seen it because he recognized it and it was easy for a man to see a familiar emotion in another man, even if that man was the King of Hell.

The cigarette dangled from the corner of his mouth, unlit. But Chiara meant something to that one. Helping her wasn't exactly a favor to him, was it? If He did Simon a favor, it was something else.

Was it that He let Simon out of Hell? That He warned him he was drowning back in the real world?

By the way, I did you a favor. So off-hand. Something rich like honey in His voice. Amusement. In the Devil, that could mean oh, so many things. How many of those things were good?

He lit the cig, sucking down a huge lungful. *Bleargh. Stale.* How long had he had this pack? Worse than last week's bread.

He wolfed the cigarette as if he guzzled water after a day in the sun. But it didn't satisfy. Not even a tingle on the tongue.

Day old cigarettes. Damn disgrace. Who knew they could expire? Out to put a warning on the pack.

Or maybe they'd gotten wet when he went through the pool. He flipped open the box and pulled one out to inspect it. Nope. Dry as bone. Shrugging, he lit it from the ember of the first before flicking the butt into the street.

He hit the pavement with a stomp, temper high up to a level of agita he hadn't known in a very long time. Right now, he wanted to get good and drunk, maybe enough to get himself into enough trouble that he'd have to charm his way out of it.

Although he had enough sense to know that it was probably a spillover effect of having recently been to Hell and back, he didn't have the sense to try to get a grip on it. Once a hoobanger, always a hoobanger.

Maybe he should try to take it easy. His head was a bit off, yet, his vision blurry in a not-really-blurry-but-something-else way. Like dubbed vocals. Not like seeing double, not exactly. There was only one of everything…but it was like seeing them twice. An overlay on everything. Double images, perfectly aligned. Truly weird shit. Buildings, street signs, people. Normal but not normal.

But then someone caught his eye, and that person was absolutely not normal.

A couple walked hand in hand toward him, laughing. The girl was cute, but unremarkable. Simon liked a little more lip and a lot more wiggle. But the man…

A silhouette clung to him like a dark shadow that had been draped over him, a shroud. One minute it was there, the next it was gone. On and off, like a flickering switch. The woman walking beside him looked absolutely normal. No trick of sunlight, no shadow cast from the nearby building.

But the guy—the shadow stuck to him as if it were a part of him. And it seemed to be growing darker.

Simon stopped in his tracks, shamelessly staring. The

couple passed by without a glance or comment. As they walked away, he felt the shadow, a little tug as if he were pulled in its wake. An—attraction. Acknowledgment.

It was too much for him to ignore. He waited a few moments before swiveling on his feet and following behind at what he hoped was a discreet distance.

Although, he'd be hard pressed to define what constituted "discreet". That wasn't really his bag.

Three, four blocks passed. The silhouette grew darker, more intense. Curiosity didn't turn into concern until he felt the warmth radiating from his amulet. That's when he knew: the shadow was not a trick of the light.

Definitely the opposite of the Light.

At the far corner, the man pulled open the door to an eatery and waited for his lady friend to go inside. Pausing, he turned his head deliberately to look at Simon and smiled.

It was a smile deep with teeth, beneath eyes that flashed crimson. A possession.

And Simon had seen it long before it manifested. Without his scrying lens.

"Uh, Mack?" Simon ducked back a step, flattening to the glass of a store front, trying to keep his voice low. "If you can hear me, I kinda need to talk to you."

"What is wrong?" Mack was instantly shoulder to shoulder beside him.

Simon bumped him out of the way and pushed him into the depths of the shop's entrance. "I found my first customer. Just walked into the corner bar."

"Why are you waiting out here?"

Oddly, the double-vision thing didn't happen when he looked at Mack. Mack was just single layer angel.

"I think I got a head start on him. But he's different. I just wanted you here."

"Whatever for?" Mack seemed puzzled. He had every right to be.

Simon had never once called Mack in for help on an

exorcism before. He was a solitary worker, not a team player. Usually, Simon spent more time trying to avoid the extra workload that came with the angel's "guidance". In his line of work, he didn't have to go looking for more work to do. Opportunities more or less presented themselves.

So. Whatever for, anyway? Just wanted the surety of a positive force behind him, he supposed. The honest response would be: Just came back from Hell and the Devil said something that worried me and I could use a friend right now.

Ha, ha, ha, no. Honesty, in this case, was the worst policy. "It's complicated," Simon said. "Just watch my back."

He stepped out onto the sidewalk and bee-lined it to the corner bar. Any minute now, he'd have a plan.

"Come on, plan," he muttered as he pulled open the door, scanning the room. "It'd be really great if you showed up now."

Nope. No plan. Looked like it was just him and his reckless impulses again.

He spotted the couple at a two-seater along the wall. The woman glanced up, wearing a completely unbeguiling expression. An innocent. The Light shined in her, compared to the blackness that sat across from her.

Simon marched up to the woman, grabbed her hand, and pulled her up from her seat. "We're going home, now."

He about-faced and tugged her straight back out the door. She'd been so stunned, she didn't even resist.

The host, though, wasn't happy. He was behind them in two shakes. Simon heard the crash of a chair being shoved out of the way.

Once outside, it was go time. He hustled the protesting woman in Mack's direction. "Mack! Distract her!"

A clouded expression flitted across her face as Mack cast his angel hoodoo on her. She wouldn't see a thing. Handy trick when trying to avoid incident—

Pain exploded in the center of his chest. Knocked backward off his feet, he hit a trash can, one of those huge solar can crushers, and sagged down the side. Dazed, Simon looked up at his attacker.

The host was cracking his knuckles, smiling. A really good punch. Either this guy lifted or—

Simon shook his head, trying to clear his vision, and ducked an oncoming fist. It crunched into the side of the metal can, denting it.

Or he had a little bit of Hell in him. That would do it, better than protein drinks and lunkhead workouts.

"Should have put your rings on first, dummy." Scrabbling out of range, he cursed himself. "That would have been an actual plan."

The amulet pulsed with a heat that spread out in front of him like a shield, pumping out more power than it ever had in Simon's life.

The host lurched forward with another swing.

Fumbling in his pocket, Simon scooted under the dude's arm, momentarily out of reach. "Whoa, pal. Hello to you, too."

The demon growled, a rumbling of syllables that sounded like metal screeching on hard stone.

"Rude." Simon shook his head in a tsk-tsk sort of way. "No need for name calling. Now, get out of that body."

WE ARE CONTENT TO STAY. The demon was openly manifesting now, misshapen skull and sunken eyes, claw tipped fingers that spread scales slowly up his hands. It glowered at him, black with darkness, eclipsed from sunlight, devil-red eyes hotly shining. *JOIN US. THERE ARE ENOUGH FOR US ALL.*

"Uh, how about no?" Rings in place, he lifted his hands. "In the name—"

Shaking its head, the demon lifted a finger over its shoulder and crooked it.

The door of the pub opened. People filed out, eyes as blank as chickens. The demon smiled and spread its hands, wriggling its fingers, gathering the men and women around it. They lurched on dragging feet, completely against their wills.

The man who stood closest to the demon started to

whimper. Smoke rose from his hair, his skin taking on a rapid and rather unhealthy-looking sunburn.

Aw, shit. Collateral damage imminent. Simon cleared his throat. "Mack?"

"I am here." The angel's voice was thick and sonorous, carrying with a weight Simon could not only hear, but feel.

Whoa. Big hoodoo. Unable to resist, he took his eyes off the demon, turning to look.

Mack was hovering. Not flying, just hovering. His eyes were ghost white and his skin had a pearly luminescence. A fog of power spread out like a gentle shockwave, bathing the gathering crowd in a soothing pool of Nothing to See Here.

Simon stared, agape. *Well. That's cool.*

Apparently, the demon wasn't of the same opinion. Dismayed at the sudden lack of obedience on the crowd's part, it began screeching again, a chorus of voices.

Mack spread his hands and pushed the growing crowd away, creating a buffer between them and the demon. The crowd remained glaze-eyed, but at least the skin sizzling had stopped.

Mack had made a No Fry Zone. No time to lose.

Simon raised his hands and cranked his rings one last time before beginning the binding chant. "In the name of the Light…"

The demon screamed, a sound of squealing pain, and fizzled out even before he finished it. Black, slithering smoke leaked out of his nose and mouth. The stink of brimstone hovered a moment before scattering on the wind.

The host stumbled forward, landing hard on his knees, head drooping.

Simon shifted his weight, one foot, the other, back. Crowd was still subdued, oddly so. Something was missing.

Chiara would have anointed the guy with a smear from her sparkly tin of chrism.

He rolled his lips between his teeth and bit. No such trick up his sleeve. Distractedly, he rubbed his chest, which was sore beneath his amulet. Fricken demon had nailed him just off-center with that one punch and the amulet had reacted, almost violently, to the contact.

But it wasn't contact with the demon's fist that had done it. It was contact with his own skin. Something new. Nothing good.

Worse yet, in the aftermath of the less-than-challenging exorcism, he felt like he didn't finish. Like an interrupted yawn.

To cover the moment, he snapped his fingers at the man's girlfriend, breaking her thrall. "Hey, I'm sorry. I thought you were my wife. No hard feelings, right?"

She blinked a few times before coming around. And she came around quickly, with a temper to boot. "Why, you son of a—"

"Okay, Mack." Simon backed away a few steps, keeping an eye on her tight fists. The crowd was coming around, too, and they all seemed a little miffed. "You can get us out of here now."

The woman lunged at him, looking very much like she wanted to sterilize him the old-fashioned way. Her battle cry was ferocious, like a cat being stuffed into a toilet bowl.

"Said I was sorry, lady." He backed away one more step, bumping into someone. Arms wrapped tight around his chest. Dammit. Outnumbered—

The ground disappeared beneath his feet. He was yanked backwards by a massive G-force. The air whooshed out of his lungs. Tears streamed from his eyes. Only lasted a second but it was enough to make him loopy and seasick and spinning on the sidewalk.

Wide-eyed, he twisted around, trying to get his bearings. Where was he? Up the street from the coffee shop. Wow.

Mack stood, watching him regain his balance, looking oddly still, oddly silent.

"Did you—you did! You mini-portaled us!" Simon danced in place, absolutely delighted. "That was so fricken cool! And that crowd control thing you did."

He slapped his hands together and walked toward Mack. "You know what, bud? We should do this more often. We make a pair. You bring 'em, I ring 'em. Wicked easy."

Mack didn't look as amused.

His somber expression made the laugh die in Simon's throat. "C'mon, chum. Why so glum? That was the easiest exorcism I ever did. You gotta admit. We did good."

The angel's eyes shone brighter than usual, his voice leaden. "I did nothing."

"Nice of you to give me the credit but, seriously." He fished out his cigarettes. "It was so much easier with you there."

The angel shook his head slowly. "No, Simon. I contributed nothing. The host did not see me and he did not feel my presence. I did not influence you or that man. All that was all you. You…and someone else."

Someone else? Er…Simon studied the lid on the box, making a fuss with the foil inside. "Who do you mean?"

"You cannot tell?"

Still no eye contact. "Tell what?"

"There was another power at work. And it was dark."

"No, sir." He pulled out a cigarette and used it to point in the direction of the bar. "The only darkness was in that host."

Mack crossed his arms and took a step back, away from Simon. Something settled into his expression. Something like…sadness. ""What have you done?"

Aw, crap. He'd never told Mack about his little field trip. There hadn't been time. The expression darkening the angel's face wasn't encouraging a confession now, either. Better to fish for answers. "What are you talking about? What's wrong? What did you see? What did I do different?"

"You did everything the same, as far as I could tell. But there was…something different, some—shadow, of a sort, bolstering your chants and your charms. That demon obeyed instantly. Not because it was you. It was as if someone were standing behind you."

"Yeah. You. Look." He made a hesitant glance at Mack,

braving the look. "You're a Watcher, right? A non-aggressor. Maybe it wasn't you but rather the Big Guy you stand for. Maybe that's what did it."

"God's power does not feel like a shadow."

"I don't know that it does or doesn't. But I do know it was a tense moment." He rubbed his mouth and looked off, down the street, away from the angel's scrutinizing gaze. "Come on. You know I've been distracted lately. Looking for her. I was worried my mind wouldn't be focused enough. Maybe that's why you thought there was shadow. I had doubt. I don't, anymore."

"Doubt is dangerous." Mack was softening, though his brows were still lowered in suspicion. "I am glad you conquered that."

"Yeah, yeah." He rubbed his palms over the top of his head, ruffling his hair. "Me, too. Listen. Seriously. Can we talk just a little about that angel stunt you pulled back there? What was that?"

Mack lifted his eyebrows with a humble shrug and set off down the street. "Influence."

"Seriously?" Simon caught up to him, feeling like he'd just had an energy shot. Excitement over having seen Mack do one of his divine doings. Elation that he'd lived through another exorcism. "Influence? That was more like, I dunno. Mass hypnosis."

"Not hypnosis. Merely a redirection of attention, a glimpse of something better."

"But that—that barrier."

"Not of my construction. Faith buffers a man and shields him from evil. Those people saw the Light, but their faith kept the demon away. All I did was behave as an angel was created to behave."

Simon mused over that. An angel behaving as was created to behave. Did angels truly exist by such simple conditions?

And what about himself? How was he to behave? As he'd been created? Was this his purpose, to chase the devils out of poor men?

He thought hard about that. To chase the Devil, right down to his lair? The full realization of what he'd done suddenly settled upon him, heavy enough to make him stumble. Mack righted him with a gentle touch on the arm, his brows knitting when Simon glanced up in gratitude.

"Simon." Mack gestured toward his face. "You're hurt."

"What?' He wiped his mouth, feeling dampness on his lip. "When?"

His fingers came away bloody.

Nothing touched him. Nothing should have come close to touching him, let alone give him a nosebleed.

He glanced up at Mack, whose expression had sunken to a most forbidding kind of concern.

Nothing good.

Bristol
South West England
a very, very, very long time ago

Zophiel stretched his wings, the sunlight creating a diffuse glow around him as he glided over the water. A new mission, a new way to serve the Creator! It filled his heart with a buoyant joy. He was an angel of God. He existed to extend His Will to mortals.

His name—"God's Spy" in the old tongue—never held negative connotation. Spying was merely watching and reporting back to those who sent him. That wasn't negative—that was simply his function. He behaved as angels were meant to behave.

He slanted his wings and drifted lower, the sunlight catching the water's surface and bouncing it back in a million mirrors. The lower he flew, the less visible he became. Angels were not visible to mortal men. It was necessary for protecting the sanctity of faith.

And the Faith was extremely interested in one particular mother-to-be. So it was that Zophiel was sent to Earth, to monitor the Enochian while she prepared to give birth. He was to watch and report back with any...anomalies.

The sight of the shoreline quickened his heart. It was rare that he was chosen for missions. This was, by far, his most important.

It would also be the first time he came upon mortals. Curiosity bubbled through him and he put new exertion into his flight.

As he approached, he spied the harbor. He would follow the water path to the city at the end, a town called Bristol. Activity churned along the water's edges. Boats of different sizes and colors bobbed near the shore, where stout wooden planks extended out in primitive decks. Hard at work, oblivious to the presence of divinity, men performed their tasks. Carrying bundles, hanging nets, climbing into their boast. This was what men did.

Men. Such amazing, dedicated creatures. Bless the Creator for so wondrous a creation. No question why He loved them so.

But why would an Enochian be here? Enochia was far more resplendent than these hardy colors and shapes of Earth. Beauty and comfort were incomparable. Placed side by side, Earth would be caustic, rough, dangerous.

Yet, an Enochian was here, in this place, preparing for the birth of her child. Not a common occurrence on Earth. One that had to be contained, if necessary.

Zophiel had been endowed with certain abilities that would allow him to easily manipulate any mortals that needed redirection. Most particular were his powers of Suggestion, Persuasion, and Assurance. Mortal men were sensitive to these influences. With them, Zophiel would have no problems herding them.

The Enochian, however, would not be as predictable. Best to let her do what she needed to do, and manage any complications that arose around her. The end game, he knew would be in getting her to go back to Enochia. But first, a period of surveillance.

At the harbor's end, he took in his first glances of the man-made town of Bristol. Completely invisible and insubstantial, Zophiel glided through the village, observing the humans in the course of their day. The markets were full and lively, a cacophony of sound and color. Men, and their offshoots of women and children, talked and bargained and traded. Enochia had none of these things. They had no need for trade.

While Enochia enthralled him, Zophiel had different feelings for its inhabitants. Angels mating with humans. It was an unsettling thought. Not having the body or the mindset for mating, Zophiel couldn't understand how the race had even been conceived. He considered them an impossibility, placing their existence firmly in the glory of the Creator, who alone knew all things.

Looking at the women, he felt no stirrings, no temptation. There was no concern that he would be introducing new Enochians to the masses. Women were only slightly discernible from the males, generally by their rounder features and the children that often clung to them. He reached out with his senses, locating his mark. She was not among these people. She was somewhere...West.

Without hesitation, he turned his back to the sun, opened his mind to her, and let her draw him in. A quarter-mile from the heart of the village, he found a small dwelling. She must be here. He could feel it.

Drifting around the corner of the tiny home, he heard an odd sound. It was peculiar—a sad sound of music that resonated within him. He peered in the window.

A luminous woman, hair the color of sunlight on wheat, clad in the remnants of Enochian silks, sat on the end of a sleeping bundle, cradling her swollen belly. Zophiel heard the sound that had drawn him in, clutched at his sympathetic heart.

She was weeping.

His prejudices vanished on the wind. This beautiful creature, far superior to all the humans he'd seen along his way, perfect even in this distended, unnatural state of pregnancy, weeping as if all hope had been lost.

It touched him in a way unlike he'd ever known. In that moment, he knew that she was one to be protected and cherished. She was one of His creations and it would be his honor to be her guardian. He vowed to find a way to bring her peace and ease the torment that caused her to weep with such distress.

His mission had officially begun.

Simon followed his feet back to Chiara's apartment.

Why? He had no clue why. If anything, that was the last place he should have gone, considering what happened less than twelve hours before.

But he was tired, like, dead to the bone tired. He was weary. And he hurt. His shoulder hurt from being tossed into a trash can. His chest hurt beneath his amulet and his brain hurt just thinking about what it meant. The only thing that didn't hurt was his nose...yet that was the part that worried him most.

His damned nose had bled so profusely he almost went to the emergency room. Almost, but not quite. Something about white coats made him uncomfortable. He'd have to be in danger of losing a limb before he went into one of those dens of misery and, even then, it would depend on the limb.

So, he'd done the practical thing. He made a pit-stop at the diner's parking lot, where his chests of magical wonders-to-behold were stored in his perpetually-parked van. Took a lot of chicory to get him there unnoticed and a heaping handful of yarrow to get the bleeding stopped before he finally dragged his behind to Chiara's place.

And all the way there, the long weary shuffle of it, his brain rolled through old footage, too tired to stop it. The memory of Kent's voice echoed in his head like a ghost, a phantom he couldn't put to rest. Too weary to ward off the memories, he surrendered to them, and allowed himself to be carried downstream by the relentless current.

"Give me your amulet, Simon..."

Kent had said it as off-hand and a guy would say "Give me your lighter." Not "give me your sole vestige of protection and kneel naked and vulnerable before me."

But he wasn't a guy asking for a light. Kent was Simon's master.

Simon obeyed, unclasping the chain and placing it on the table between them. It took every bit of his will to do it. When was the last time he'd removed it? When was the last time he'd trusted someone enough to even let them look at it?

Why did he feel so powerless?

He kept his eyes on it as if his gaze would maintain some tactile contact. The pendant wasn't large, or extravagant. The size of a nickel, maybe, with a double ring of three hearts each, the inner ring resembling a shamrock. Lucky charm, his mom had said. He supposed it had worked, considering he was standing here, looking at it, despite all he'd done to try to get himself obliterated.

His mother had worn it and gave it to him when he had her committed. He had worn it ever since, a sign of her love, his betrayal. Two things he never wanted to forget. It was one of the few things he'd taken with him when he left his life in Belmont behind.

It meant everything to him now. As a son, as a mage, as a soldier against the dark.

And it was the one thing that protected him from what he both hated and feared most...

Simon shook himself out of the reverie as he dragged himself up the last flight of steps, sliding along the wall toward Chiara's door. The lock clacked open at his approach, loud enough to bring him all the way back into the present.

He shuffled through her door, too exhausted to mind the wards while they did their little pat down. The amulet warmed a few degrees hotter than usual, probably because it sensed he had worn himself to complete defenselessness. He stroked it with reverence, a grateful thought that at least something still had his back.

Pulling out the poultice he'd packed into his nostrils was a complete nightmare. Chunks of weed and dried blood stuck to his nose hairs, making its extraction a new kind of painful experience, complete with a wimpy sting of involuntary tears. Not seeing a wastebasket, he tossed the remnants of his nasty cure into the fireplace.

The fire roared, devouring the bloodied yarrow with a shower of green sparks.

Uh, oh. He slapped himself on the forehead. *Stupid, stupid man. Just fed blood to a mystical fire—*

A chuckle sounded from the fireplace—a deep, sultry laugh he recognized at once. The sound crawled up his spine and brushed the back of his neck, making him shiver.

And he knew. He *knew*.

The nosebleed hadn't been an accident. It was a blood price.

That exorcism had been simple, annoyingly so. He didn't have to even perform the whole ritual. It was like the demon knew where he was headed and finished it for him. No demon should ever want to do that.

That demon was nothing special. It had referred to itself as "us", right? So it had no particular identity. Plain old minion rank, one of a billion nameless hoard that clumped together like slime cells on a stagnant pond. Nothing special, nothing new, nothing different than the hundred he'd pulled out of people in the past.

So, it had been him. *He* was different.

He sank down onto Chiara's ratty couch and glared at the fire. He should have known. Didn't the Morningstar tell him he'd done him a favor?

And, by the way, what the hell? Why would the Devil make him a better exorcist?

Power. A whisper slithered through the room, echoing over and over.

He sat up, hastily scanning the parlor, the stairs.

Giving the fireplace the side eye, he slipped his hand into his pocket, fingering through his charms. When he brushed against the silver crucifix, the whisper deepened into a disapproving rumble.

Not in my house, you don't.

"What do you want?" He twisted, scanning the room, the ceiling, not knowing where to point his voice. Bravado from a beggar. At least he didn't sound like a terrified twelve-year-old.

The very same that you want. To find my daughter.

Simon rolled his shoulders and sat back, the lumpy cushion denying him comfort. His tattoo twinged as if an ice cube slid across it and he rubbed it absent-mindedly. "How does a stupid nosebleed get that done?"

I cannot see her from my vantage. I need eyes on the mortal plane. You are to be my envoy.

"Shit." He rubbed his hair back hard enough to hurt it. "No, sir. Not your envoy. That's a direct violation of my ethical standards."

Ethical, indeed. Lucifer issued a dismissive noise from deep in His throat. *Those so-called standards permitted you to venture to my own realm to recruit my assistance.*

Simon grumbled. Not like he'd known exactly who was going to pick up the phone when he dialed. "Yeah, but—"

Ignorance of the law is not an excuse to break it. More than a little amusement lightened His voice.

He could hear the Devil smiling. And the Devil smiled only when He was winning.

Talk about a losing battle. Simon sighed. In for a penny and all that. "Fine. What are we dealing with?"

You carry a piece of me within you. It is tied to your power. Not your soul, I assure you. The voice took on an arch tone. *I prefer those to remain...organic. Ensures a pure harvest. But your magic—that I can work with.*

"And the bleeding?"

You are a mortal. Mortals are not meant to wield such immense strength.

Good old-fashioned cockiness rolled to the surface. Simon bit back retort after retort. Wouldn't be a good idea to mouth off to this guy.

Mmmm. Pride. I think that is one thing I do like about you, Alliant. Your swollen, grotesque pride. It is admirable.

Morningstar was reading him. Simon bit down on his lips and forced himself to think of a blank sheet of paper and a single droning syllable, trying to empty his mind. Hard to do with the tattoo pulsing with a happy little heartbeat of its own. Damn thing was responding to the Devil's power. Not good.

All it did was earn him a wave of condescending laughter.

That's the spirit. Do that. Hide your thoughts from me. But do not defy me, Alliant. You will do what you must to find my daughter, or you will pay a price greater than a handful of blood.

The fire suddenly flared out, swelling, crackling, sending out a shower of spitting embers before shrinking down, down, down to orange coals, which pulsated with a sullen heat like a distant heartbeat.

The room felt empty but for himself, once more.

"Okay," he said, hoping no one was listening at this point. "Guess I'll just go to sleep, then."

Would his favorite room still be there? He climbed the stairs and peered around the corner, down the long hallway. The very end was completely shrouded in blackness. Kind of comforting, that. Didn't really think seeing that door would be conducive to a good night's sleep.

About halfway down, one of the doors stood open, a warm light spilling out into the hall, softening the darkness with an inviting glow. His room. He breathed a sigh of relief. Maybe something good could come out of all this bad, after all.

Carefully, he paced toward the open door, slowly and deliberately, wanting nothing more than to flop onto the big pillow-top bed with its pillows and memory foam, but fully expecting trap doors to swallow him or a creep-show beast to pop out.

The edges of his senses tingled, kind of like a blip on the radar. His amulet pulsed once, a spot of heat, a bump up in his protections. Something was up here. Something he hadn't noticed before. He paced past each of the rooms, their doors closed, and leaned to listen. Nothing.

Another door, another scrutiny. Nothing.

The door to the room catty-corner to his stood slightly ajar. Although that room was dark, it buzzed with a ward that felt like a burr bush, scratching at his senses, snagging his attention. He paused in front of it, examining the ward's power signature. Something not exactly *unknown*—

When he turned to look at it, the door slid shut with a sullen click. The anticipation of something unpleasant switched off. Whatever was in there didn't want to be seen.

Fine by him. He wasn't in the mood for another intrigue. He shrugged, not having a clue, not wanting one. Giving the door a stern glance, he waved a finger at it. "And stay in there."

The distraction dispelled, he drew a deep breath and focused on the spread of light that poured from his room. It was like an open embrace that beckoned to him.

Now, everything was peaceful up here. Quiet. Right. Just like it had always felt when she was around. Maybe...

He shook his head. He wasn't silly enough to think she was in there. But he was human enough to hope, and lonely enough to wish.

Simon dallied in the bathroom only long enough to peel off his soiled clothes and scrub the old blood off his skin. The bed was as soft as he'd remembered, the pillow just as fluffy. As he sank into the warmth and the soft and the comfort, he let himself remember her scent, and pretended she was there.

It was as close to together as they were going to get. It would be enough to keep him going.

It had to be.

12

The next day, Simon hit the street feeling like a brand new penny. Washed, shaved, fresh as a pressed shirt. (Which, incidentally, he wore. His room had a closet, he'd discovered, and the closet had clothes in it. He hadn't even needed to finish rinsing out the bloodied shirt he'd left soaking in the sink. Wicked convenient.)

The only remnant from the previous day was a sore arm, as if he'd taken a wand hit. But he hadn't even touched his tattoo. Probably not a good sign.

He brushed it off, reminding himself that he had used magic. That tat was the hub of his power. It only made sense that it would feel used.

The solid night's sleep had worked a magic of its own on him, sharpening the fuzzed-out corners of his psyche. It would take an extraordinary breakfast to patch up the blood loss. He frowned. Rainier was not going to like his omelet order.

Spinach would be weird enough a thing, considering the entire diner knew he was carnivore first, meatatarian second. But the black sesame seeds and beet juice would have the cook dialing 911. A side of liver and onions and they'd be sending in the white coats as back-up.

Shoot. Maybe a stop at the drug store for some gummy multivitamins was a better idea. That way, he could stick to his beloved breakfast meats. To avoid suspicion, of course. Discretion was his specialty.

Or so he pretended until later that afternoon, when he realized he was being followed.

This was the city, for crying out loud. The streets were lousy with people. Couldn't swing a pendulum without hitting someone. People were always following, no matter which way a guy walked.

But they didn't usually carry the shadows with them.

Maybe it was a trick of the light. The sky was spotty with clouds. Could just have been overcast.

But that guy at the bar had shadows. They hadn't been a trick of the light. Why would these be?

A casual glance over his shoulder showed blots of dimly lit people moving amongst the ordinary folk, each honed in on him. When he blinked hard, the sight shifted, flickering back and forth between normal eyesight and the shadowed overlay. Dammit.

"Uh, Mack?" He coughed into his cupped hand, trying to not look like he was talking to himself. "I think something is happening."

He crossed the street and headed north, focusing on his periphery. The shadows followed, deepening with each passing minute, the crowd growing. He led them like a piper through Hamlin.

On a whim, he paused in his tracks, spinning on his heel. Each of the pre-hosts stopped in time with him, giving him a level, dead-eyed stare. The second sight flickered, revealing maniacal grins in the shadows.

Oh, bad, bad, super bad. This time, he didn't care who overheard. "Mack! A little help here?"

Nothing. No wind, no mellow voice, no itch of angel feathers along his nerves. No Mack. He searched the skies, looking for the sun. When he found it, his hopes dimmed.

The sun blazed high above a thick ceiling of cloud on the horizon, solid except for a slit through which the sunlight streamed down in a golden veil. A Jacob's Ladder, far to the north.

Dammit. Angel business. Mack wouldn't be coming.

It was up to him.

Tapping his mouth, he sifted through a dozen possibilities, all of which ended in bad. His blood tingled through his extremities as adrenaline pumped through his system, tunneling his vison and muffling his ears with the boom of his pulse.

Not panic, he told himself, breathing through pursed lips. *Not yet.*

But soon, if he didn't do something. He'd never faced an ambush before. And this was looking like a fricken big one.

He paused at the corner, just a beat, deliberating. Okay. Ambush by a bunch of people who looked like that last host had, the one with possession prodrome. And him? No plan, as usual.

He was getting used to going without one. Didn't mean he was any better at it.

A deep breath, a look around, a survey of the area. Three blocks away was a small warehouse with a fenced-in lot. Buildings spread out, not usually a lot of foot traffic, no ley lines. As good a place as any for a holy showdown.

By the time he reached the gate, he knew he had a good dozen pre-hosts behind him. He could feel each one of them. Collectively, they emanated an energy that felt like a change in the humidity, a palpable pressure. Keeping his back to them, he paced to the center of the lot.

They streamed in behind, their breathing audible and disturbing.

He walked a clockwise circle, dragging his left foot in the dirt as he did. When it was complete, he leaned over and spit onto it. A brief glow zipped around the edge as the circle awakened.

His tattoo winced with a lance of electric pain as it did, like he'd whacked his funny bone. It hurt so massively that it was difficult to decide if it even hurt at all. And this wasn't even a blooded circle.

The pre-manifesting hosts drifted out around him, their shadows deepening, their mumbles growing more audible, more aggravated.

"Yeah," he said. "It's a cheap circle, I know. Beggars can't be choosers, right?"

The shadows stopped flickering, his sight sticking itself in Dark Mode. Arm throbbing as if he'd just taken a massive wand hit, he surveyed the lot. He didn't need his scrying lens to know these guys were all turning into the Walking Hell. His tattoo did all that for him, whether he wanted it or not.

Damn it. Why? Why does Lucifer's power have to be so damned useful? With every trick, every boon, he was coming to appreciate it more and more and that didn't make things any easier. It only blurred the lines he'd spent years sharpening.

Light, good. Dark, bad. Used to be easier than black and white. But shortcuts like this made him think that, even though it was Dark, it was serving his purpose.

There was nothing in Heaven or on Earth that was good nor evil. It was all a matter of intention, right? It wasn't the power, or the advantage, or the charm. It was what a man did with it that counted.

Without hesitation, he slipped on his thumb rings, twisting them into position, feeling them catch when they got there. He pushed up his sleeves, like John Henry getting ready to pick up his sledgehammer. The cool air hit the tender skin of his tattoo, a brief soothing before the sting of the dark charge hit, the power rolling off the manifestations surrounding him.

He scanned the crowd, thirteen by his count. Their demons

hadn't emerged yet. The old Simon would have been more concerned for a gang mugging or a cult intervention.

But this new layer of flickering sight, the back-and-forth between normal and Dark—was this what Chiara lived with? Was this how she saw the world, every day, the simple light of a person destroyed by the potential of Darkness? Where was the hope, the optimism? Not that he'd ever had an overabundance…but the thin supply he possessed was diminishing by the hour.

Quick flashback to that day on the bus when she spied that punk who'd been ready to manifest, long before Simon had even suspected something bad was up. Chiara had a jump on the kid's impending possession. She'd been ready to go before the kid even turned.

Now, he was wielding that same upper hand. He was the one who was ready to go.

Maybe it wasn't as doomsday as he'd initially thought. He grinned, now, and swiveled his head slowly around, evaluating each one. The hosts were in varying stages of possession. Not all going to pounce at once.

Old Simon would had said: good on that. Divide and conquer. Take each one out, one manageable demon at a time.

New Simon was…well, a little disappointed, truthfully. Things would go a lot smoother if everyone was on board together.

Well…his grin widened, baring teeth. *The rules had recently changed, hadn't they?*

He sized up the situation. Never before would he have attempted a group exorcism, let alone this hot mess. The thing to do was corral them, somehow, and grab their demons all at once. But first, he needed to get their attention.

Certainly, Old Simon would never have provoked such a dangerous mob.

"Oh, well," he muttered, rubbing his thumbs and fingers together. "Out with the old."

He tugged the chain around his neck, drawing the amulet

out from under his shirt, and dropped it upon his chest, in full view.

Provoked wasn't the word. The man closest to his left snarled and hissed like a wet cat, eyes sparkling like poisonous rubies.

"Ah. Hello, you devil. Who's first?" With an offhanded flourish, he pulled his wand free of his watchband and twirled it between his fingers like an 80s rock drummer before pointing at them. "You? You, sir? Who?"

The hosts, red-eyed and ready to blow, kept their distance. They swayed on stilted legs, their breaths ragged, choking on their own brimstone.

He glared at them and smiled a mad smile. "Cowards."

Gripping the wand hard, he nailed his tattoo.

He yelled in anticipation a split-second before the hit, nerves breaking loose. The scream that followed the hit was real, and raw, and shriveled his manlies tightly up against him with a dull ache.

An expanding ring of power sliced out like a shock wave, smacking into the hosts, locking them in place as if they'd been electrocuted. They manifested as one, like microwave popcorn. Just BOOM! BOOM! BOOM! Full-on possession, every single one.

The air inside the circle tasted like a car fire. His nose stung. His eyes burned.

And he laughed. Laughed at the pain, dwarfish in the rush of the power he had at his beck and call. He laughed and raised his hands. The blue arc of magical electricity that spun between his rings was so much thicker, so much brighter than he'd ever conjured. The power rumbled down his arms. His voice came out like a lion's roar.

"In the name of the Light, I draw thee." He slowly turned, hands out, the power stretched between his rings like a rope of living, twisting taffy. It crackled with a ferocity that echoed out, bouncing off the fence, the warehouse further back. "In the name of the Light, I bind thee. In the name of the Light, I cast thee back into darkness. In the name of the Light, I—"

The demons screamed, held in thrall within his orbit of power. They screamed, writhing in agony, and they hung upon his every word. Waiting.

Simon's head felt wide open. He looked into the sullen eyes of each host and knew the name of each demon screaming within them. He saw the desperate souls trapped inside them, tortured within the vortex of demonic possession, each twisting in the hell of his own body.

He saw the infinite well of Hell's power embodied within the grip each demon had upon its mortal victim.

And Simon was bigger than all of it.

"Aw, heck," he said. "Who am I kidding? I command thee. Thou shalt do my will."

He stared down each demon, each minion cowering in the light of his rings and the storm of his power. Gritting his teeth, he leaned into the magic and put every ounce of his strength and his will into each word.

He called out the name of each demon, once no more than an archaic name in a dusty old grimoire. Now, each name had a face and a personality and an existence. He called out each name, commanded its obedience, and drew it out.

A ghostly image lifted up out of each body, the shape of a demonic minion that squirmed, helpless to disobey Simon's call. Rage. Such rage—it could singe his eyebrows if he got close enough. Rage rolled off each demon as they flapped and shrieked, piniomed to their hosts, desperately trying to hold onto their purloined mortal shells.

Simon wind-milled his arms, up and out, the light stretching between his binding rings. As his hands came up together in front of him, the power pulled into a tight ball.

There's the wind up. Here comes the pitch—

He hurled that power at them, launching it like a holy RPG. "Go back to your place below!"

The ball of power arced through each host, electrifying and tethering them like too much Spielberg and not enough sleep. The demons were ripped out of their hosts, shattering into sulfuric sparks. They sizzled out as one, the smoke hanging like a sooty veil over the alley, over the body of each man and woman who'd collapsed, falling into a crumpled circle around him.

Laughter seized him like an alien force, maniacal laughter that threatened to liquefy his brain if he didn't let it out. Standing in the center of a ring of unconscious bodies, he threw his head back and laughed out his delirium, his incredulity, his conquest, his relief. Too many feelings for a mortal psyche to comprehend all at once. It translated into a roar of belly laughter that drowned out any concept of comprehension.

He couldn't process it. He didn't care. Dropping to his knees in the dirt, he threw back his head and laughed—

And for the briefest moment, Simon's vision was cast over by a sheen of silver, his eyes glinting like a jet plane flying straight into the sun.

Bristol
the distant past

Zophiel remained ever at Luminea's side.

True, he, an angel, was invisible and could not touch the earth, could not communicate with her. That mattered little. After all, it was not his right.

He was content to watch. Sometimes, she talked out loud to herself, nonsense about daily chores or what would she wear to market that day. He would talk back to her, even though she couldn't hear him. It didn't matter. Nothing was silly or trivial as far as she was concerned.

Watching the beautiful and despairing Luminea, her struggle to reconcile her fate, her broken heart, her loneliness—it affected him. His mission was to watch, yes? To be a guardian, surely. But she was a divinity, stranded alone in a sea of incognizant humanity. She needed someone.

And as her time to give birth grew closer, her anxiety increased, and he knew he had to take action. Zophiel went to the village, sought out a midwife, and used Persuasion to get her to take a cart out to the western farms.

She found Luminea in the early stages of labor and thanked God's providence profusely for leading her there.

Luminea didn't seem so much piously thankful as politely cautious. But once the pains arrived, she was less about caution and more about making it through.

The labor was long by the midwife's standards, if her frequent exclamations were truthful. But the delivery itself was uneventful and easy. Zophiel hovered at Luminea's head, whispering Assurances. The child slipped free from her body, strong lungs and bright hazel eyes. As Luminea held the babe the infant's eyes often strayed beyond her face toward his own, as if she sensed his presence.

A unique child, befitting of so remarkable a woman.

Luminea and her child became another fixture in that mundane world. She was clever and talented, finding ways to use her natural powers to make craft, earn coin, all without raising suspicion of witchcraft or devilry. The humans of that time had been very suspicious of such things.

So odd, Zophiel would muse; they prayed every day for miracles and signs of God's blessing but here was a true example of divinity living amongst them in the mud and the sun and the raggedness.

And they'd hang her by the neck if they knew the truth.

She sewed canvas sails for the sailing captains, with needles that never broke and fingers that never grew tired or sore. So quickly did she produce them that she soon became the most sought-after craftswoman.

Her sails never tore, never failed to find fair winds. Enochian magic, of course. And while the captains all proclaimed there was something of very good luck in her sails, they never once thought she was the true source of it.

Bristol thrived as a port city. It would become a place of power. Luminea sewed relentlessly through the night, her mind turning and twisting through plans she would set in motion now, seedlings to grow, great mighty trees to last eons. And she would control it all…

All these things she shared with her now-teen-aged daughter, who learned in time how to handle the heavy canvas, how to slick the thick twine with wax and with magic to protect against fraying, how to command the canvas to yield to the point of the needle, how to spread the Enochian magic through every fiber.

That last part, she fumbled. The final blessing, a great undertaking to be sure, was simply beyond her strength.

"You will grow, dearest," Luminea would say, her voice like harp strings coated in honey, bright yet mellow. "All things work in balance. You do good work with your hands. Your mind will follow."

Zophiel's wings would hum with his approval, Luminea's esteem as a beautiful soul rising even higher in his regard. His heart swelled with it.

But not everyone felt the same way about her. Especially not the rival sail makers whose livelihoods had suffered greatly at her success.

One such man was known for his coarse, blunt ways. A lifelong sailor himself, Jon Burton was accustomed to surviving on the wretched sea, tossed about by the water's merciless moods. And he cared not for women, unless they were buxom and accommodating and willing to leave by morning.

Luminea was not his kind of woman. She was a threat to his business. And, Zophiel had heard him say on several occasions, it was time she remembered her place.

Burton's work orders becoming scant, he took to drinking ale at all times of the day, thoroughly inebriating his judgment and impairing his senses. His favorite tavern was one that sat close to the harbor, favored by sailors and merchants alike. Zophiel could see him watching her though the open windows each day as she passed, carrying the day's deliveries.

Zophiel felt the hate radiating from him, his turmoil and loathing and desire to right what he believed was a terrible injustice. He was on guard against that one.

One afternoon, having delivered her wares, Luminea walked past the tavern, her purse heavy with coin, her mind on the next project, the next stage of her plan. She had been too distracted to notice Burton had stepped out of the doorway just on her heels, and followed her with a seething intention blackening his heart.

Zophiel saw him. He always saw.

When she turned the corner, he rushed closer and elbowed her against the wall.

"You don't belong here, woman." He growled his words, his rancid *breath causing her to twist her head away in disgust.*

Her courage was that of a lioness. "I belong where I choose to belong."

"Then choose your proper place. On your back, or next to your kitchen fire. Not here, amongst men of the sea. Pretty faces are good for only one thing here, missy. And if pretty faces hang out long enough, they get what they're good for."

She responded with a slap, a strong swing that rocked him back a pace.

Zophiel felt the man's rage spill over and knew she was in trouble. But...what could he do besides watch?

Desperately he looked around. She needed help, an intervention. Only one other man was in the vicinity, an elder. He would not be much use.

Unless...he had divine help.

Zophiel came down behind the elder's body, hovering over him, closer, closer...then closed his eyes and pushed his way inside him.

He sucked a loud breath, the sensation dizzying and terrifying. He felt the body around him, his eyes only seeing as a mortal, his ears hearing only as a mortal. Yet for all the limitations, there was heat, there was blood, there was a stout heart that beat in his breast.

There was ground, beneath his feet.

He wanted to sing with it, to fly with exhilarated wings.

A cry brought him back to his senses. Luminea. He tried to fly to her. No wings. He ran, clumsy and knock-kneed, rounding the corner to where Burton had Luminea's hair bunched up in his grimy fist, her pale cheek reddening from a blow.

Zophiel descended like a madman, his anger slick and fast. He grabbed Burton by the shoulder and spun him around to face him.

Startled by the old man's sudden appearance, Burton released Luminea and she fell back against the wall.

Burton's face was a mixture of anger and astonishment. "Taylor," he said, a warning in his voice. "Best be along. This does not concern you."

Zophiel smiled, thin and menacing, and struck him.

It was a simple gesture, a quick extension of his arm, a balled fist, aimed for the center of the brute's face. A simple gesture, powered with the strength of an avenging angel.

Bone cracked beneath the impact, bright blood splashing over his flesh.

Sound, color, wetness. So many sensations. Zophiel couldn't keep track of them all. Over the rush of sensory intake was the pounding of a human heart—the heart inside his chest—

Burton fell to the ground, keening, holding his face.

Zophiel stood over him, a titan.

"She does not concern you, little man. And if you ever cause her as much as a single thought of worry—" He leaned down, lowering his voice to a quiet menace. "I will know, and I will show you your place, which is very close to where you are lying now."

A long moment passed between them, disbelieving defiance etched in the deep lines of Burton's spattered face. Sullenly, the conquered man pushed to his feet and staggered off, without as much as a look in Luminea's direction.

Zophiel stood watching after him, not so much seeing as feeling the still-alien sensation of corporeal form. The sunlight on his skin was a prickly glow, true heat. The zephyrs from the harbor were a constant play upon his skin, moving his thin hair in a constant caress. Humans lived this, each moment, each day of their tiny lives. How did they stand it?

And then another sensation overwhelmed him, and his thoughts ceased. Luminea had flung her arms around him, hugging him and thanking him for his rescue.

Oh. Oh, that. Bliss, defined.

He closed his arms gently around her, lost in the embrace. This—this touch, her body, her scent. She had a scent! It was clean water and sweet flower, overlay with a slight pungency of the canvas she had carried. He could smell the sunlight on her hair, the faint wisp of perspiration that was a nectar to his brand new senses. It was intoxicating.

So much so, that he lost his grip on the man's body and was cast out.

Once more, an angel. Suddenly devoid of the marvelous riot of human senses. He was crushed by the loss.

He followed Luminea home, still clinging to the memory of her flesh against his, and venerated each step of her foot, waiting until the day he could repeat his venture.

He didn't wait long. He took the man's form again a few days later, this time only to chat. There was no embrace but there was a touch of her hand upon his arm as she thanked him again.

Mat Taylor was a widowed fisherman who seemed to pity the young mother and her struggles to earn a living in a world where men dominated. He admired her craft and felt she deserved a chance.

But he was elderly, and worn out from a hard life on the sea. Zophiel found it easy to take his body at will, even if only for a few moments in passing. He looked forward to her walk to the harbor each day, hoping for a few moments longer to feel the sun and wind, to catch the scent of her skin. He craved it to the point where he could think of nothing else.

Weeks passed in this fashion, a miracle in itself. Zophiel learned to tell the passage of time while spent in corporeal form. Time itself—another wonder to behold!

But time was not kind to mortals, especially not elderly mortals whose bodies had been weakened by the passage of time. Zophiel realized that, each time he took Taylor, the body was more frail than it had been the time before. His possession caused physical damage.

And one day, Zophiel found he could not enter the man at all. Taylor was simply too weak.

The next day, perhaps, he thought. He could go one day, let the man rest and heal and grow strong enough.

It would not be the next day. There was never another next day for Mat Taylor.

When they passed his cottage, Zophiel found only a black banner above the door, the sounds of weeping within. Taylor had passed away during the night.

Luminea wept, her sadness at losing so kind a friend nearly breaking her heart, and shattering his in the process.

He hovered over the tiny gathering at Taylor's grave, emanating blessings of Peace and Comfort down upon Taylor's family, upon Luminea and her daughter.

He, too, was distraught. His actions had shortened the life of a mortal. He'd gone against his Master's Will.

But he knew his desire to be with Luminea was greater than any guilt he felt about causing harm. He had crossed a line—and it was not a line an angel should even know existed.

Simon woke up in a ditch.

Literally, a ditch. And not a clean, comfortable one, either.

What the frick was digging into his back? He pushed himself upright and twisted to look behind him. A shoe. Jeez. It wasn't even his. Could have been worse, considering he was lying in a ditch with absolutely no idea how he got there.

What time was it? Oh, yeah. He wore a watch. Good for something more than holding a wand.

Wait. His wand. It wasn't there.

Simon was on his feet like he had springs in his ass, wildly patting himself down. A familiar shape in his back pocket. He swallowed his heartbeat down and forced himself to breathe.

Climbing out of the ditch, he scanned the area. Sounds of brisk, steady traffic. A highway. Must be I-83. He squinted and tried to read the green overhead sign.

"Wait a minute," he mumbled. Did that say Towson? As in

ten miles outside Baltimore? "Gotta be fricken kidding."

How did he get here? Didn't remember. Last thing was that bangin' gang exorcism. Then, just memory mush.

Then a ditch and a shoe. *Wow,* he thought. This was rough, even for him.

He pulled a smoke and lipped it without lighting it, more out of habit than hunger.

Looked back at the signs again. Yep. It was 83, all right, and a lot farther from town than he liked to walk. He checked the rest of his pockets, finding a wad of crumpled bills. At least he came with cab fare.

He plucked the cig from his lips and tucked it back into the pack. The cigarette caught when he tried to slip it back in and nearly bent. Little buggers were a terror to put away. Not that he'd ever tried that before.

Wait. Did he just try put a cigarette away?

He stared down at the half open pack in his hand, not quite believing even as the facts lined up and presented themselves for inspection. He hadn't had a decent smoke since he came back through the pool.

And he didn't want one now.

Oh, hell no. That son of a bitch of a Devil. He did this.

He frowned, feeling more put out than he'd ever felt in his life.

"Lucifer." A shudder went through him, one that gripped him in the gut and made him nauseous. He felt...violated. "You just don't mess with a man that way."

Well, this sucked. Amnesia and cigarettes that failed to quiet the hunger. Talk about being stranded. He clasped his hands and hung them over his head, at a nearly-complete loss, watching the traffic speed past.

A sudden sharp lance of pain in his left arm made him curse. He turned his arm over and stared, agape.

His tattoo. It had been altered.

A new ring had been added around the periphery, a Celtic knot that wrapped around the outermost ring. He turned his arm to the light and squinted. The detailing was exquisite. Actually kinda cool.

Kinda bad that he didn't recall being in a tattoo parlor. Was this why he woke up so far from his neighborhood? To get ink? And why would he alter this one instead of working on the sleeve he'd started on the other arm?

This runic tattoo had been a two-man job of Kent's design— and he hadn't met a second man worthy enough of the job in a very long time. Hopefully, whatever he did to it didn't screw it up.

He lifted his arm and peered closely at the knot work, whistling his admiration. Expertly done, he had to admit. The entire knot was made of a single line, patterned and twisting. There was only a single break where the two ends met. A snake's head, mouth open, jaws wide, tiny fangs ready to bite the tail.

He stroked the edge, noting the absence of redness or swelling that was the hallmark of fresh ink. As he ran his fingertip over his skin, a prickly sensation started, feeling like goosebumps on a sunburn. It bunched and pinched around the entire tattoo. But it wasn't the weird sensation that made his mouth hang open.

It was the way the ink *moved*.

The snake came to life beneath his touch, sliding and squeezing its knotted body around the edge of his tattoo. It encircled and ensnared—

And he knew—God help him, he knew. He knew where it came from and he knew that it was responsible for what he'd done. What he remembered doing, anyway. He had no idea what he'd done in absentia of his mental faculties but whatever it was, the tattoo was probably responsible for that, too.

There was only one guy responsible for the tattoo.

"Oh, Lucifer." His voice was low and ragged. "You son of a whore, you."

Was this the favor Lucifer had said He'd done? This ring of ink that took him to a whole new circle of power? The tattoo never had this kind of strength on its own, never. And he sure as hell wasn't a natural mage.

Just a purveyor of parlor tricks, petty charms, chants and prayers and the wishes of a man who believed in magic. That's what his power had been, right up to the point when the Devil picked up a needle and scarred his soul.

His magical power wasn't just boosted—it was augmented to new strength, new depth. And a tiny voice niggled at the back of his brain that the reason it had been such a snap to exorcise a gang of demons at once wasn't because he was more powerful.

It was because he was different.

Before, he had to fight to make them abandon their hosts. He had to overwhelm them with surprise and magic and faith. But this last time—he just told them what to do. Those demons had recognized an authority and they obeyed him. As if he were a traffic cop, redirecting demons back to Hell.

He hadn't needed the extra show of power. That had been simply a bit of panache.

Simon chewed his lip, feeling more than a little guilty. It was spectacular, though. Wicked fricken pisser.

He staggered away from the ditch and sat down on a nearby cement blockade, watching the traffic zoom by. His nerves had stilled their noisy jangling. That little touch had awoken the snake, and that tiny activation had quelled what the cigarettes didn't.

Oh, no. He closed his eyes and let his head droop back. He was in the shit, now. Bad enough the wand hits had been needed more and more frequently. He knew he had a...slight problem. He knew it had been getting harder to satisfy the craving.

"Say it, Simon." His voice was drowned out by the drone of the unending stream of cars. Didn't matter. He could hear it. That's all that mattered. "Addict. You're an addict. But you knew that. You've known it for a long, long time. So why all of a sudden are you going Twelve Steps on yourself? Why now?"

He knew *why now.*

He scrubbed his mouth with a cupped hand. The answer was obvious: he'd just tasted a new drug. He tasted, and he devoured, and he cross-faded to the point of oblivion before waking up in a fricken ditch.

The cigarettes—they weren't stale. They were useless. He hadn't wanted one since his trip to the other side. Lucifer had taken that addiction away. Some favor. The Devil was the king of all nicotine patches.

Simon needed the nicotine addiction. It helped keep the other one at bay. But now—

He swallowed against a tongue made of cotton, his stomach twitching and every nerve starting to itch like boredom times ADHD times infinity squared. Hungry? Yes. No. There was only one thing.

Without cigs to keep the gnawing need muffled, he needed something else to abuse. He hovered his palm over the bend of his elbow, the slight heat of his hand like a lewd suggestion.

Great. Manual stimulation. Magical masturbation.

He closed his eyes, unable to look, but more than ready to touch himself. A new kind of low, one he couldn't smart-ass his way into justifying.

Maybe he should just get back into the ditch and save everyone a lot of time and trouble.

"Oh, Lucifer," he whispered. "You son of a bitching whore, you."

"Zophiel." Luminea's voice held a sharpness usually reserved for the under staff. "Have you heard a word I've said?"

"I apologize, madam." He did not resent the correction. Having lead so long a life, his kind was prone to becoming wrapped in reveries. Time flowed oddly around divinities, and the border between past and present was sometimes too thin to maintain proper separation. "I'd been lost in thought."

She softened her expression. "No small wonder. We've seen a lot together, you and I. Her being here brings much of it back."

"Indeed it does, madam."

"Well. We are not the sentimental type, are we? Daydreaming about the past is no way to secure a future. Have you seen her?"

"I have looked in at her, madam."

"My daughter." Luminea lingered over the words, savoring

them. "I never thought she'd be here, or be so beautiful. I am not shallow, of course. She would be my daughter even if she weren't pleasing. But it does improve the aesthetics, does it not?"

Zophiel clasped his hands behind his back. There was only one he found beautiful. Any other was substandard. "Beauty is appreciable in many forms."

"Even when it's useless?"

There was that tone, that undercurrent that perpetually lurked in her shadows. Luminea was intelligent, beautiful, talented, devious. But there was something else to her. Self-loathing. Self-depreciating. She took on the faults of others and bore them like crosses. She punished herself for the sins that others had inflicted upon her. It turned a rage into a monstrous entity, roiling beneath the surface, unfathomable.

Generally, she directed that rage to building and creating and gaining and amassing. But not always.

Sometimes, she used it to destroy.

"Beauty is never useless," he said. This was a time for redirection. She, of all creatures, should venerate herself as a paragon. "Especially not when it is entwined with talent and promise."

"Oh, promise." She smiled, her eyes still cold. "Yes. There is so much promise in this endeavor."

"Yes, madam." Zophiel kept his expression still. She was listening. A simple *yes, madam* kept her listening. She preferred obedience, the feeling that she was in control. "I believe you will achieve great things in this. You will finally obtain your peace."

She nodded, a sharp dip of her head. "Good. I like the sound of peace. It has long evaded me. I will enjoy it, I believe. You must, too."

Hard to decipher the meaning of that last part. He dared a glance at her, needing a read of her facial expression, knowing it would likely be unhelpful. Her expressions rarely tipped her hand.

Zophiel was not concerned. He knew her intimately,

deeply, completely. Her meanings would all be clear in time. But it did help, knowing who she was and what she has always wanted.

"Has she seen you yet?" she asked.

He shook his head. "No, madam."

"I don't expect her to recognize you. Not in that get-up." She waved a finger at him in an up-and-down sweep. "No matter. I have every reason to believe she'll figure out exactly who you are. But I need you to remember one thing. She is my daughter. She is not the girl you remember, which makes your job easier. But she is still my daughter, and I need her."

Zophiel made no reply. Instead, he stepped over to her and kissed her forehead, smoothing her hair gently. Her scent was intoxicating, even after all these years. His body reacted the same exact way whenever they were close. He let his lips linger, breathing her in.

"Go." She turned away. "This needs to be done."

He felt her absence immediately, her warmth suddenly gone. No matter. There will be a next time. The thought of that was enough to sustain.

He would do anything she asked just for another chance at *next time*.

Anything.

16

Another day, another exorcism.

The black smoke fizzled up and out of the host, flitting away like an acrid breeze. Simon rubbed his nose. Never got used to the smell.

Or the nosebleed. The bright red smear on his knuckles matched the disquiet that slow-roasted in the pit of his stomach. A price.

Petty price for power of this magnitude.

He scrubbed his hand against his side, glad he'd started wearing dark shirts. Easier to hide the occasional hemorrhage.

But black t-shirts didn't do anything to hide the purple bruises in his nail beds. Those started showing up the day before. And his toothbrush had been an unsettling shade of pink this morning. Anyway.

He sized up the host, wondering if he needed to call 911. Maybe not. The guy looked like he'd passed out standing up, but he was breathing. That much was okay.

Something else caught his notice.

Looked like the smoke lingered. Weird, considering the breeze than continuously flowed through the streets of the harbor city, as if it breathed with life of its own.

He squinted. No. Not smoke. Too thin, too straight, too well-defined. His second-sight showed the possession was resolved. The demon was exorcised. Nothing but tired, messed-up people left in that body.

But there was something else. Looked like a string. Simon walked around, peering behind him. A black string that came out of the center of the guy's back, between his shoulder blades. It trailed up into the air, straight up like a string on an invisible balloon, disappearing into the heights.

"What the hell?" he whispered.

The host roused, shook his head, looked strangely at Simon, and mumbled.

Simon shrugged. "You okay, pal?"

The guy scrubbed his eyes with his palm, blinking hard. "What was I doing?"

"You just asked for directions to Westminster. Did you hear anything I said?" Simon squinted his eyes and gave him a suspicious look. "You sure you're okay?"

"Yeah, just...sorry. And thanks." He walked off up the street, not in the direction of Westminster, and banged a right around the corner. That string went right along with him.

Simon heaved a sigh. Curiosity would kill him one day, he knew, but still.

He counted to three before he followed, hurrying to catch up. The host had already made it to the end of the block, tethered to that funky black string.

Not smoke.

Had to be bad. Had to be. He scanned the sidewalks, scrutinizing the people. There. Across the street. There was another black string, this one tied to a twenty-something in a snap-back hat and droopy basketball shorts. The kid glanced over at Simon.

Wait a second. Simon knew that face.

It was the kid from the bus. The ride-along with Chiara. The one who'd been possessed by one of Balazog's a-hole minions.

He wasn't possessed now. In fact, the second-sight thing added a gentle glow around his face. Chiara's chrism. That had to be why Simon saw Light within him now.

Well. Looks like Heaven left a stain, too. Good to know the Devil wasn't the only one leaving a mess behind.

So. Two previous exorcisms, and both had a weird tether on them. So, bad. Had to be.

Bad was getting to be a regular thing.

Simon followed the punk kid, chanting Mack's name in a low desperate litany, across town and up through Fells, trying to hang back enough not to be noticed but not enough to lose him.

Mack joined him halfway to Butchers Hill.

Terrible name for so quaint a neighborhood. Little bit foreboding. Hopefully, things wouldn't turn out as pessimistic as he anticipated, because things usually did. Oh, well. Maybe if he took up different work, he wouldn't have to prepare for things always going to hell.

"Okay. There, guy in the red shirt and stupid hat." Simon nudged Mack with his elbow and pointed with an unlit cigarette between his fingers. At least his smokes were good for something, considering how expensive they were these days. "See it?"

The kid was only half a block ahead, strolling along the tree-lined street as if he hadn't a care in the world, talking on his cell phone. Mack leaned his head closer and followed the line of sight along Simon's gesture.

"Nothing that should alarm you, if you were capable of seeing it." The angel looked down at Simon, a curious tilt to his head. "What is it that you see?"

"I don't know. A rope? A line? Something."

"I see only a touch of grace upon him. But not a rope or line." Mack shook his head. "I will inquire. But I do not anticipate I will receive good news."

Simon fiddled with the cigarette. Still so odd to be playing with it and not smoking it. "Me, neither, but I'm getting used to it."

"You should not 'get used to it'. That is pessimism and pessimism is the enemy of hope."

That was refreshing. Pessimism was the enemy of hope? And here all along he'd thought it was just him. "So are black string trailing off former hosts. I don't like it. It's like the darkness was exorcised, yeah? But it still has a grip."

"Perhaps it isn't darkness." Mack folded his hands and took up his default stance, the serene monastic sway. "Perhaps because the soul has been saved, it has a special link to the Light, as if the Shepherd is watching and keeping track."

"Then why isn't it a gold string or a rainbow of something shiny and happy looking?"

Mack gave him a sideways glance. "As I said...I do not anticipate good news."

"Yeah. But, don't lose hope, bro." He clapped the angel on the shoulder. "That would be bad, coming from you."

"Yes, it would. I must investigate. I will return when I have information." The angel stepped back a pace, melting into the fog of his wings, leaving Simon with an unlit cigarette and a chest full of pessimism.

Nothing to do but wait and wonder what would happen next.

Simon woke up curled on his side, knees drawn tightly to his ribs. That was the first clue that something wasn't right. Usually, he started the day spread-eagled on his back, deep in the fluff of the mattress, as if he tried to press every possible inch of surface area into the impossible comfort of the pillow top.

The second clue that something wasn't right was the stomach cramp, the tight ache that vice-gripped his belly and lower back. He'd barely made it into the bathroom in time.

Perhaps it was a repercussion of the previous day's exercises. The stroll home from Butchers Hill had been nothing short of phenomenal. It played out like a scene from a movie, full of effortless exorcisms. Six or seven of them, at least, and none requiring more than a point and a command.

Go back. That was all. No ceremony, no thumb rings, no precise intonation invoking the Name of One more powerful than he. A man across the street, his black tether swelling on engorging power, his shadow growing. A woman leaning on the windowsill of an apartment overhead, eyes flitting to hot red upon seeing Simon. The driver of a bus who had flipped his sign to NOT IN SERVICE despite having a full load of passengers. Simon just stepped in front of the bus, pointed at the flickering shade of the pre-manifesting demon and, like an annoyed school teacher, said "You. Out. Now."

And the demon sizzled out. The driver regained control of the bus and swerved barely missing Simon, but back on course.

All the demons sizzled out, every single one Simon encountered. He pointed and commanded and continued on his way, a merry bit of bouncy music playing somewhere in the back of his head. The nosebleed was no worse than usual, so bonus right there. He wasn't even tired by the time he'd gotten back to the apartment, and he should have been completely knackered. Long walks were the enemy of a seasoned smoker.

Bonus bonus—he didn't black out and wake up in a ditch. Maybe he was getting the hang of this new thing. Falling asleep with a sense of satisfaction made for sweet, optimistic dreams. Then the pain woke him up.

Looked like he was paying for it today.

When he at last felt like he could get off the toilet, he stared down at the water a long, long time before flushing. The pool of dark blood made him realize something wasn't simply not right.

Something was terribly, terribly wrong.

This blood price was escalating. Wiping the cold sweat from his upper lip, he avoided meeting his own gaze in the mirror. Would he be called on the tab before he found Chiara?

It took him a long time to get down the stairs. Pretty bad when you had to stop to catch your breath on the way down.

He slid bonelessly through the gap in the front door, unable to push it farther than the initial sticking point. Overhead, the sky was thick and sullen with dark, unspilled clouds. The usual balminess of the harbor air felt flat, stale.

Dropping down on the stoop, he propped his elbows on his knees, hands clasped. Didn't feel like it was going to be a swell day.

His suspicions were confirmed when his lifted his head and looked dead into Mack's stare. The angel stood on the sidewalk, statue-still. His expression seemed set in stone, heavy and resolute.

Simon groaned. "You don't look like you got good news."

"Did you notice the Ladder that went up to the North a short time after we parted ways yesterday?" There was an odd tightness to Mack's voice, as if Simon's answer didn't matter.

He warily eyed the angel, unsure where things were headed. "Yes."

"So did I."

"And…?"

"And I hadn't been Summoned to attend." It came out like an accusation.

"Well, that's weird." Simon swallowed another a wave of nausea, half-concerned that another bloody trip to the can was imminent. "Right? 'cause your expression is making me think it's weird."

"It isn't weird, Simon. It's unthinkable. Any time a Ladder goes up, every Watcher upon the Earth is Summoned. It is our right. It is our duty. It is our reward."

"So…" Simon's stomach had lumped up like he'd swallowed a wad of cement. He was pretty sure at this point it wasn't the blood price making him so uncomfortable. "Was there a glitch?"

"A glitch? You might call it that." Mack nodded and flicked his glance away. "Or, you might use concise language and say that I have been determined currently ineligible for summoning."

Too many long words in one sentence for a guy who was bleeding out on the inside. Oxygen deprivation made a guy dopey. "Ineligible. Why?"

"Well, perhaps that is the part you can explain. Would you explain why you have tainted my purity?"

"Whoa, pal." Internal hemorrhage or no, he was not sitting

down for something that heinous. A man had to stand for something. He swayed when he stood, but didn't fall down. "You need to back that right up. If I was going to taint someone's purity, she wouldn't look like you. And I'm pretty sure she'd already be tainted—"

"Stop it!" Mack advanced on him, grabbing his collar and hoisting him up straighter. "You always do this. You make jokes about things that are not the least bit humorous. Do you have any idea what this means? My purity, tainted? Ineligible for a Summons? And why? What did you do, Simon?"

The angel released him and backed off, his storm relenting, and pointed a sever finger at him. "Because you did something. Too many new strange things happening to you at the same time that I have been shunned."

Simon gaped at him. Shunned. That was never a good word. Too many images of banishment and exile and rejection. It was the ultimate punishment for a creature that thrived on connection, on communion. An angel shunned was an angel denied access to the very reason for its existence.

And it was his fault. All of it.

How did he even begin? With an apology? With a flat-out admission that he'd screwed up worse than he ever had before? With the truth?

Mack seemed closer to emotion than he'd ever appeared before, true emotion. Angels could be snotty and they could be bossy and they could be downright judgmental sometimes but there was one thing they should never, ever be.

Heartbroken. Disappointment so weighty, so galactic that, at this moment, Mack looked like his heart had been broken, busted, and blown to oblivion.

And it had been all his doing. Simon felt deflated, felt like he was nothing more than a sorry stack of failures. He sank back down, the gravity of his sin crushing the last of his strength. "I should have told you when it happened. Shit, I should have told you before I even did it. But I didn't have a choice."

"You are human," Mack said, his teeth gritted. "You always have a choice."

So much heat. Angels had no choice, no freewill. He knew it was a touchy topic with Mack, who followed orders with explicit precision. But never before had his friend made him feel like he'd squandered his own will.

He lowered his eyes, chastised. "Sometimes, it doesn't feel like I do. Like that day. I was getting nowhere, Mack. Even with that vision. Might as well have been a figment of my imagination because I was nowhere closer to finding her. So, I looked for help. Her kind of help."

"And?"

"And...I summoned her father."

"Her father being...?"

"A demon, Mack." He chickened out at the last minute. Would it make a difference? Would it change anything by telling him who the demon was? "I summoned a demon because I couldn't think of anyone else willing to help me find her. And all this—the nosebleeds, the new...talent, your shunning—it's my fault. It's my fault you aren't getting the Heavenly memos."

Several long moments went by, Mack saying nothing. Would he leave? Would he bring God's swift hand down upon him? But neither happened. With a sigh, Mack sat down on the stoop next to him.

"There is no fault. You did not intentionally create this situation." Mack eased up on the attack, seeming to regain some of his benevolent tolerance for him and his unending screw-ups. "This is an effect. An unhappy accident. But you did choose to contact the demon. And you choose to continue using this power."

"To do the right thing." Simon spread his hands, palms up and pleading. "I've knocked out more possessions in the last week than I have in a year. Real results, victories for the Light. Isn't that what counts?"

"Simon, if you sell your soul to bring about world peace, the result would be a wonderful, beautiful thing. But you would not have a soul. And you would be lost. And the loss of even one soul is a terrible wound upon the heart of the Light."

It was so hard to counter a statement like that. He'd known Mack a long, long time and there were some things that he held sacred. Mack's reverence for a soul's redemption was one such thing. "So...what do we do now?"

"We follow the lead I have found."

"What? A lead? Why didn't you say so? Can you trust the source?"

The look Mack dumped on him was as close to *are you fricken kidding me?* as he'd ever seen the angel get. "It is the same source who informed me of my current designation. She, too, does not put faith in coincidence. He has shared news of a particularly suspicious disturbance."

"Okay. That's good, right?" Bad news, but good that he got it, he supposed. Mack mustn't be actually shunned if the other angels still hang out with him. "A real lead from a bona fide source. What's the plan? "

"We leave at once to investigate this disturbance. I have examined it, from afar. The energy feels suspiciously like your compatriot."

Simon didn't like the repetitious use of the word *suspicious*. Considering the situation with his current state of reprimand, Mack was exhibiting more than the usual amount of bias. The angel was entitled, he'd give him that.

But still. The word painted Chiara in a negative tone. It flushed through his veins, a hot infusion of resentment.

He had no right to get indignant now, not after all Mack had done. Certainly not after what he was enduring, all at Simon's doing. "What are you waiting for? Let's go."

Mack stood and folded his hands over his abdomen, slowly shaking his head. "I think we should discuss some things first."

"No. Not with a fresh lead. Delays could be catastrophic. Talk later. Portal now."

"Simon—"

"Listen, Mack." He pushed to his feet. "It's already taken

too long. We're running out of time."

"But I do not know—"

"You know where she is. That's enough." A cramp doubled him over and he swallowed, hard, the taste of pennies in the back of his throat.

Mack righted him with a touch on his shoulder. "You are in no shape to travel, Simon."

"Are you kidding me?" He wiped his mouth with the back of his hand, wiping it on the seat of his jeans without looking. "Just get me there. I'm not the one who matters anymore."

But that was only part of the truth. Truth was, time was running out.

For Chiara. And for him.

Simon sat on the curb, trying to hold his forehead in place. A chunk of sugared ginger made the back of his tongue tingle, the peppery sharpness seeping into his copious saliva.

Dammit, the sun was too bright. What happened to that nice, miserable cover of gloomy clouds?

Maybe Mack had even held back his hair while he yacked into the gutter. Always seemed like the type that would. At any rate, Simon was grateful someone had his back. More often than not, it felt like too many others were aiming for it.

The strength of one true friend outweighed the threat of a thousand enemies.

He swallowed another mouthful of ginger-lanced spit, his stomach slowing its roll. A few minutes more and he'd be almost right as rain. Right enough to walk upright and not get picked up for public drunkenness, anyway.

"Are you quite sure you are well, Simon?"

Simon waved at him as if he shooed a slowly-moving gnat. "Never better. You know I love a good portal."

"You never suffered ill effects before." Mack hovered nervously. "Your physiology is unbalanced."

Unbalanced? Might say that. "Just a little woozy."

"Is this nicotine withdrawal? I've never seen you go through it. Where are your cigarettes, Simon?"

"Ugh." Simon swallowed a wave of sea-sick, the thought of menthol-flavored smoke making his stomach bob. "Why? You want one?"

"No. They are harmful. A deplorable habit, but not one I ever imagined you to relinquish."

"Well, we all change and grow."

"No." Mack shook his head pensively. It wasn't an insult; it was, simply, an open assessment, a truth he already accepted. "You do not change and grow. That is contrary to your nature. You are rather...set in your ways."

Simon squinted up at the angel, who was back-lit by the much-too-bright sun. "You might be impressed."

"I'd rather not be. Your surprises often result in explosions."

"They do not! And that was, like, one time." He paused. "Two. Okay, two times. Jeez, Mack. When are you going to let that go?"

"I cannot forget. I am incapable."

"Thank God it's not your job to forgive and forget."

A trace of a smile ghosted across Mack's face. "You are correct. But there are advantages to possessing infinite recall."

"Sucks to be you. Forgetting is the only thing that lets me keep living."

"That is truly regretful, Simon. I am sorry for your sad outlook. And sorrier still for your condition. On your knees, retching. But, at least, not patting yourself down for your cigarettes."

"Still on that?"

"I simply observe." The angel looked him up and down

once more. "You are behaving oddly."

"I'm having hot flashes. Does that count? Man." He wiped at the dampness on the back of his neck and tugged at his collar. "Is it me or is it muggy?"

Mack lifted his chin as if scenting the air and nodded. "The humidity is different."

"So, I should ask where we are."

"Savannah."

Savannah. As in..."Georgia?"

"Yes. Savannah, New York is much—what?"

Simon stifled the end of his groan and rubbed his eyes with both hands. "Just *ugh*. Rebel demons. Can't wait. Well, don't just stand there. Give a hand."

He bit back a groan as Mack helped him up, the change in equilibrium doing little to maintain the small progress he'd made with his stomach.

"Can you walk?" Mack braced Simon's back with a steadying arm. "I can feel...something...to the northwest."

"Chiara?"

"It has that same quality, the disturbance. I would have liked to deposit us closer but my instinct is to be wary. Whatever it is, it is more than your friend. It is something that would know if we had opened a portal in its proximity."

"I suppose so, considering her mother is Enochian. Close enough to angel, right?"

"Enochian?" Mack lost the nursemaid vibe and went on angelic alert. "Are you quite sure?"

"As sure as I can be. Chiara said her mother is Enochian, and—" He cut off before saying *her father is the Devil*. Still pretty sure Mack didn't need to know too much about that part. Or anything at all about that part. He'd already spilled enough beans on the subject. Why did he feel like he had a dirty little secret?

Oh, wait. It was because he did have one. The dirtiest of all dirty little secrets. Making deals with the Devil. For an exorcist, it didn't get any dirtier.

"And I'm pretty sure that's who has her." He rubbed his eyes, glad of an excuse to avoid Mack's scrutiny. "Do you think that's what you're picking up on?"

"It could be. It has been a very long time since I've been exposed to an Enochian on this plane. It could be I simply have grown unfamiliar with the timbre of their power. I didn't expect it to be quite so…resonant. Yet, not." Mack lifted his shoulders in a movement that looked almost like a shrug. "Perhaps I have been Watching you for too long. I am losing my basis for comparison."

"Maybe ask around. You know. Your buddy."

"No." Mack narrowed his eyes and scanned the far-off. "I cannot beckon to her. She comes to me of her own will."

"Well," Simon said. There it was, the use of the word *she* again. Mack never referred to his compatriots with any sense of gender, and certainly never mentioned them having a will of any sort. *Another holy mystery of the angel kind*, he thought. But there was no time for sleuthing it out now, no matter how nosy he wanted to be. "No news is good news. Right?"

"Rarely so. This is a complex time. There is always news." He sniffed, a disdainful sound. "Do you need more rest, or shall we proceed? We have a distance to go."

"How much of a distance?"

Mack reached beneath his tunic, tugging out a small pouch. Carefully, he loosened the strings and tipped the bag over his cupped palm. A fine stream of glinting power poured out, piling in a gel-like mound. When he'd accumulated a teaspoonful or so of the shiny stuff, he stowed the pouch again.

Simon watched, mouth half-open in an eager smile, drinking up every gesture. It was a rare treat to watch Mack do angel tricks, apart from that noisy heraldic Metatron junk.

In fact, he could count the number of times he'd seen Mack use chrism on one hand, with two fingers tied behind his back. This was the real deal. No card tricks or lucky charms. This was divine magic, even if *magic* was too trite a term.

One of these days, he'd get him to lend him that bag of his.

The power had to be massive, a straight-shot of divinity. Just a fingerful. That's all he needed. Then they'd see who was the boss...

He shook his head. *Wow. Reality check, Simon. A little power hungry?*

Mack lifted his palm to shoulder height and smeared the air in a broad swipe. The chrism spread out, forming a veil that hung between them. With an index finger, Mack poked the veil, which shimmered and quivered beneath his touch. Glittery sparks spread across it, dots and lines and squiggles.

A map. A fricken magic map. Simon clapped his hands once and whistled, earning a very strange look from a woman passing by. Sometimes, he forgot no one else could see Mack. He must look totally nuts, standing out on the street, talking to himself.

"We are here." A dot pulsed and glowed bluish-white, like over-bleached teeth. Hovering his hand, Mack finally indicated a second glow above it to the right. "We must go there."

"What's that, a boat?" He scratched his head. "No, wait. I'm on the wrong side. Show me the state borders."

Mack tapped the veil, straight lines of laser glow outlining the familiar, if backwards, shape of Georgia.

"Atlanta." He bit his lips. "A little farther than a walk, I'm afraid."

"You look disappointed."

"Yeah, well. I won't be the only one."

"What do you mean?"

Simon sighed. "Zoom in on that map of yours. Show me this city."

Mack tapped the lower dot once and it expanded wide, a series of squares and long lines that were unmistakably Savannahan. "Yes?"

"Now Google 'bus station'."

He would have laughed at Mack's sudden dismay if he wasn't so overcome himself. Dammit, he hated buses. At least he still had some ginger left.

But not enough for two. He hoped angels didn't get car sick.

Bristol
the distant past

Luminea lay sleeping. She did not sleep often; when she did, it was merely for appearances or for the sake of passing a long night. Zophiel had hovered anxiously, his heart conflicted. It had been so long since he'd been inside a human body and he fretted, obsessed with the desire to feel her near him once more.

His obsession had culminated in a terrible decision. He would appear to her in a dream.

It was a sin for him to even think upon it. Angels only carried God's message, not their own. And this message he wanted to deliver was his, and his alone.

He blessed her with an oracular dream, the kind angels used for God's messages. Her eyes were bright with hope when she saw him.

"Luminea, I am the angel Zophiel. I have been sent to watch over you

since you came to this land."

"Zophiel! Can it be true? An angel? Then I have not been cast out of Enochia. Do you come to take us home?"

Her voice held such eagerness, such yearning that he immediately regretted his decision. She thought her exile was ending.

"I do not have the power," he said. "I am sorry."

Her face crumpled a moment with tremendous disappointment.

He hurried on to spare her from dwelling too much upon it. "But I must give you knowledge. It was I that appeared to you as the fisherman Taylor the day he saved you from Jon Burton."

There. It was out. He waited a moment, allowing her to absorb the truth.

"You appeared to me. As a human." She narrowed her eyes. "Angels cannot do such a thing. It is forbidden."

"Yes," he said. "But I forbid any man to lay hands upon you to cause you harm."

"You forbid? Not God?"

He lowered his eyes. "It was a decision of my own making."

"But angels are servants."

"Something which you are not." Even in this dream state, he could not keep the heat out of his words. "You are not some lowly wretch who deserves harsh treatment. You are to be protected. You are to be appreciated and cherished."

"By you?"

"If you will have me."

She seemed to think that over. "Can I actually do so?"

"Do what?"

"Have you. Have you as you appeared as Taylor."

His heart leapt. She was thinking exactly what he had hoped she would.

"Yes, I can. And this is what you must do, if you truly wish it to be."

He gave her careful instructions, knowing she would remember every detail, hoping against hope that she wanted what he wanted. The quick gleam that settled into her eyes as she listened sped his hopes onward.

When he ended the oracular dream, she awoke with a gasp, looking wildly around. He panicked. Would she pass it off as an inconsequential dreaming?

She got up to check on her daughter, who stretched in front the fire, deep in a sleep of her own. When she spoke aloud, he nearly fell.

"If you are real, Zophiel, and if you have spoken truly..." She crossed her arms, looking up at the ceiling.

He floated over her, gazing back into her eyes, pretending she could see him.

"Then she is not to know. You must pass for one of us. If you cannot do this, then I will not seek you." Luminea went back to her bedroll and pulled the weave over herself before lying down. "But if you can do that," she whispered. "Then I will seek you tomorrow."

With that, she rolled over and closed her eyes.

She did not sleep.

He watched, as was his place to do, and tried not to think what it would be like to stop watching and start doing.

The mirror shimmered and rippled, heralding the approach of a visitor.

Chiara was on her feet in an instant. Her apprehension from being trapped in this doorless prison like a caged bird prevented her from sitting still. Never had she known this state of agitation, a jangling of her senses that was most discordant.

This must be what mortals meant by *feeling jumpy*. It was quite unpleasant.

Her mother stepped through the glass portal, followed by another, a man of burly build whose power rolled like a thunderstorm trapped in a pretty blue-skied balloon. Nothing to see on the outside, but beneath...

Oh, there was something beneath. And it wasn't right.

The discordant power made her skin itch, adding to the already distressingly-high level of anxiety. She eyed him warily.

"What is this, Mother?" Chiara stepped behind the couch,

wanting to put as many obstacles between them as possible. Yes, it was telling. Yes, she betrayed herself by showing how she felt. But something more than body language politics was key, now. Self-preservation. "You employ hired thugs now?"

"Why, my dear," Luminea said, phony cordiality in her voice. "You remember Zophiel."

"That...is Zophiel?" Self-preservation forgotten at the sound of so familiar a name, Chiara peered intently at the man. "No, no...it cannot be. Zophiel has blond hair, green eyes. Taller. Not so..."

She searched for a diplomatic word. "Stout. Or red-headed."

"Appearances are superficial." Luminea's tone was...hard to interpret. It sounded very much as if she were displeased with him, somehow.

"You look nothing like the Zophiel I remember, but it's more than that." Chiara shook her head, wearing a tiny frown. "You feel nothing like him."

"Why would I?" His voice held the slight drag of a Southern accent. A secretive smile tugged the corner of his mouth, sly and dangerous.

No. Zophiel's voice had been sonorous, smooth, English. This was not the same Enochian she'd known as a child. He'd been a foster parent to her, a tutor, a disciplinarian. She knew Zophiel as well as she knew her own mother. "Why wouldn't you? Mother looks the same and I haven't changed very much—"

"My dear." Luminea's voice took on an annoying tone of patience, sounding much like a parent lecturing a small child. "Zophiel requires an anchor on this plane."

"I don't understand. You don't need an anchor. Enochians possess enough mortality to be recognized by the physicality of Earth."

Luminea smiled, the same secret smile Zophiel wore. Mirrored upon each of their faces, it became a threat. "That's correct."

"What are you not saying?" Chiara struggled to piece together the conversation, force it to fit the confines of common sense. "I don't understand."

"You don't need to understand," Zophiel said. "You only need to accept."

His tone held so much familiar dark authority that she could remain still no longer. Fight or flight. She retained enough sense to know she couldn't fight something she didn't understand. And so, the second option became the only option.

Chiara went for the shimmering mirror, too fast for mortal eyes to track. It was a speed that her Enochian mother did not possess, a part of her otherness. The strike of a serpent. The flash of a lightning crash. Sometimes, her father's gifts were most convenient.

She made it past her mother easily but at the mirror Zophiel appeared, blocking her way.

He didn't even seem to have exerted himself. One minute he was on the other side of the room, the next he was standing in front of the mirror, arms crossed, eyes hooded with disapproval. The next, he was a wall.

A wall that was more offense than defense. He raised a hand and hit her with a wave of invisible force that made her stumble backwards.

"You." She gasped for breath, the force of his impact having hit her square in the chest. Fisting her hands, she planted her feet, bracing against another attack. "You portaled. Enochians cannot do that."

He smiled, cold and cocky. "You are not as foolish as I'd assumed you had become. What am I?"

Wild with panic, she sought Luminea's face. "Mother—"

"No," he said, his voice low and gravelly. "Answer me. What. Am. I?"

Her stomach roiled into a tight cramp, her body itching as if insects burrowed beneath the surface of her skin. She knew. Her gut knew.

Her senses had prickled at his presence from the moment

he came in. Only one race set off those particular alarms. Only one race that could open such clean portals.

Angels. Zophiel was an angel. The realization of who he was, who he'd been all along, made her physically ill. She shook her head, swallowing back a nauseating mouthful of saliva.

"You cannot be. All this time—you were family, you—" The horror of all that was unfolding threatened to drive her mad. This creature had been masquerading as an Enochian ally, her mother's closest companion, Chiara's own mentor. A surrogate father for the one who could not be there for her as a child. Zophiel had been friend and family and protector.

He'd tutored her in the way of Enochian magic when she was an adolescent. He possessed a patience her mother did not; Chiara's otherness was a defect Luminea could not always handle with grace. Zophiel recognized the uniqueness Chiara bore upon her powers and encouraged her to accept them, accept herself. It was like he knew a secret about her, and that secret was safe.

All of it. A lie. The parts of Chiara's soul that ran darker and deeper than the rest ignited like an oil slick under a match. Betrayal did not sit well with her father's blood. Nor did treacherous angels who slipped free of the noose of judgment.

If one angel was to pay the ultimate price, so must they all pay.

Her hands boiled with impotent heat. Had she not been trapped in this heavily-warded prison, she'd be brandishing fistfuls of hellfire. And, oh, the things she would do with it. A correction would never be as spectacular as the one she hungered to execute right now. "You abomination."

"Come now." Luminea never moved, never even turned her head. Instead she lifted one hand to inspect her manicure, never seeming the least bit bothered by her daughter's display. "That's no way to address a being of the Light."

Chiara spun to face her. She, the architect of this whole wretched farce. "An angel, Mother? You commandeered an angel?"

"No, dear, I didn't. Why would I need to commandeer anyone?" She got up and slinked over to Zophiel, stepping behind him and running her hand across his chest. "He's here because he wants to be. Although generally he retains a much more alluring form."

Luminea's pretty mouth tilted with disapproval. "Ah, well. As soon as we find the right body, we'll make the adjustment."

Zophiel never took his eyes off Chiara, never lost the cocky smile. "Yes, madam."

Chiara covered her mouth. "You wretched being. You stole a human's body. Do you not care about the torture you inflict upon that man's soul?"

"You worry too much about men's souls." Luminea bit off each word. "Speaking of which…don't you have something to do, Zophiel?"

"Yes, madam." He bowed his head to her before zipping out of sight. Another effortless portal. It grated on her thinning nerves, knowing he was in full possession of his power when she was cut off from her own otherness.

Luminea sauntered over to the side table and tilted back the lid of the serving dish. Picking up a slender silver fork, she speared a slice of peach and took a delicate bite.

"The finest of fruits. Like sunlight upon the tongue. We had nothing like this back home in Bristol, did we? Only what the fishermen brought in, or what we could grow in our miserable dirty fields." She took another bite, closing her eyes, savoring the taste. "This city is built in sunlight. The gleaming spires, the sweet winds, the hedonistic perfection of flavors. This is a paradise to be plundered."

Chiara strode over to the table and shut the serving lid with a *thunk*. "Don't change the subject, Mother. What are you doing with him? How can you stand to be near him, knowing what he is?"

"He is loyal." Luminea frown, disapproval etching into the downturn of her mouth. "Unlike one's own child."

Chiara ignored the jab. "He's a skin-rider."

"And I need skin." Luminea's voice was sultry with undercurrents.

"Ugh." What a repulsive thought. For her, physical intimacy first required absolute trust—and very few had ever performed in that capacity to her satisfaction. It was difficult to overlay her particular emotional perspectives upon a creature as deplorable as a mutinous angel. "Please say you don't mean what I think you mean."

"Do you think I've been celibate? Please." Luminea slid her palms down the sides of her body, emphasizing every curve. "This body is literally a gift from God. Not one to be wasted. I have needs."

Oh, this was not a conversation she wanted to have with her own mother. No, no, not at all. She hurriedly turned her back, wishing it could shield her, stop her ears. "I don't want to be talking about this."

"Zophiel has been my companion for centuries, Chiaroscuro. He has never abandoned me. You once thought of him as family."

"Because I thought he was family. He lied to me. He masked his true self and pretended to be someone I loved and trusted." Chiara sat down on the edge of the couch and folded her hands. "I know the truth, now. I cannot trust him in any capacity."

"Why? Because you've learned that Zophiel is more than just my assistant?"

"No. Because I learned what he really is. Mother." Chiara lowered her voice to urgent tones. "What he does is treacherous. Even by my standards."

"Treacherous?" Luminea seemed not to care if anyone overheard. "Don't be silly. This is the mortal plane, dear. There is no treachery here. In fact, the rules are sketchy at best. And rarely enforced."

"So says the Enochian who cannot die on this plane, thus evading judgment."

"You're a fine one to judge, girl." Luminea lifted her chin.

"What happened to your precious sense of neutrality?"

"It's perfectly intact. As are my morals. As is my certain knowledge that the Divine have no right upon this plane. He should not be here. You should not be here."

"I cannot be elsewhere." Luminea crossed her arms and turned her back on her, standing to gaze out the windows toward the silver horizon.

"No," Chiara said. "You refuse to be elsewhere."

"I *cannot* be elsewhere." There was a subtle but sure emphasis to that word, matched with a downturn of her icy eyes. "Do you forget? We lived here on the mortal plane all your life. We made our home on this Earth. We lived amongst mortals, assumed their habits, their cultures, their traditions."

Something of sentimentality in her tone made Chiara get up and join her at the window. With a light touch upon her arm, she urged her mother to look at her. "We lived, Mother. It's what people do."

"We are not people." Luminea patted her hand once, a resigned sort sadness giving way to something stronger, something harder. What had been soft and pliable in her voice was now forging itself in steel. "We are not mortals meant to muddle through this filthy plane like meat bags with an expiration date."

Luminea backed away, framing herself in the brightness of the broad window, back lit by the glint of sunlight off the city surroundings. "I am Enochian. I am of the Light, the purest of planes below the Celestial. Descended from angels. Angels! Creatures of clarity and crystalline grace. Unsullied by death or dirt or…despair."

"My point, exactly. You've never been content here. Why stay?"

"Because I cannot be elsewhere!"

A familiar guilt settled over Chiara. Long before she'd left home, she blamed herself for her mother's separation from her friends, her family, her home. Zophiel had played no small role in that, she realized, with his secret insinuations and his disappointments in her failings as a daughter of Luminea. It was what spurred her to seek far-off lands, what drove her away from her mother.

She'd long ago come to the conclusion that her mother abandoned Enochia because of her. The unwanted child, her dark heritage. A stain upon an Enochian's name. "So leave this all behind. You don't need all this—this fortress, this city. We lived simply once, remember? I'm not saying we need to live in the Middle Ages again, but we can live cleanly. Like when we had that little piece of land near Bristol."

"Yes, I remember Bristol. Knowing we were safe so close to the water. And I remember when they built that bridge—no magic, no power, just the work of their dirty hands and sore backs and sheer determination to conquer that water. Such a shame to see it replaced by that boring, iron thing. So like people. Taking monuments of toil and heartbreak and replacing them with cold, unfashionable strips of metal. It's not the same. Bristol isn't the same."

"So don't go there. There are other places, simple places. The shorelines here are mainly all built up now but in Canada there are vast wildernesses, and many great lakes and rivers, close enough to water—"

"Water?" The look Luminea tossed at her was heavy with contempt. "Do you think water is enough to protect us now? You know it cannot. You've proven it cannot."

"Not us." Chiara turned her head. "But I don't need to be protected."

"Of course, you don't." Luminea's tone turned to glass, cold and sharp. "You are his, aren't you? Your father's daughter."

"That is not what I meant."

"Doesn't matter anymore" Luminea said. "We are here. We will stay here. I don't need water to surround me. I have power."

"Power?"

"Yes. My empire." Luminea clucked her tongue. "Come now, dear, you can't say you haven't noticed. I've done quite well for myself."

"Yes, you have." Chiara rolled her eyes. "This is very beautiful. The prison you have me in is quite exquisite."

"Don't patronize me. You may not be able to appreciate what I've done but, I assure you, I do not miss home."

Chiara remembered the tales her mother had told her about her home in Enochia, wistful bedtime tales of light and grace, fairy tales and happily-ever-afters. She'd never understood why they didn't go back, not even after she'd been on her own and made telling discoveries about herself. "Not even a little?"

"You can't miss a place that doesn't want you." Luminea stood and tapped the side of her eye, blinking. "And why should I miss it? When this whole world is open?"

"Not for you, Mother." Enough was enough. Whatever mood possessed her mother of late, it could not be excused. Chiara had long believed that when she left home, her mother had gone back to Enochia. Apparently not. Living on the mortal plane was no crime, but consorting with a angel such as Zophiel—that was inexcusable. "I mean it. What you're doing here—it's not right. Zophiel should have been dispatched ages ago."

"Dispatch Zophiel? Why would I do that? Do you know how difficult it is to find good help these days? And not just the help. What he can do with his hands—"

"Mother!"

"I'm talking about massage, dear. Really. Not all of us dream in the colors of perdition."

The colors of perdition. What a bleak thing to say. Perdition was one of those words one seldom heard on this plane, not unless someone was referring to ultimate damnation. To hear it from her own mother's mouth…it weighed in her chest, a palpable ache.

She lowered her head, unable to face her mother. Although Zophiel had been the one to make her believe such things, she'd held onto the hope that the negativity had been only his, a secret. To hear it now, from her own mother, was grievous.

Chiara felt small and discarded, a vulnerable child, so great was her re-animated shame. "Is that what you think of me?"

"Of course not." Luminea seemed not to notice the anguish that twisted Chiara inside. "I'm just saying. Zophiel knows me. He understands me. I don't want to have to re-train someone new every fifty years. It's exhausting."

"He's an abomination." Chiara knew how many times she said it, the word would not alter her mother's perception. What Luminea believed, was. End of story.

"Zophiel has no choice. That is the prevalent theme here. There is no choice. Not for him. Not for me. And, certainly, not for you." Luminea approached the mirror, pressing a finger to the surface, activating the passage way.

"There's always a choice, Mother."

"You have had the luxury these many years, my love, of living in the best of both worlds. Well, I haven't. I only had this world. I have had to make do. And, well," she said, her voice lightening into an arrogant laugh. "If I haven't just. So. You should sit back and enjoy your quarters, and the service, and your new situation because, my dear, this is an empire, and it takes a family to run it."

She stepped through, her last words distorted as they echoed through the rippling glass. "Welcome home, child."

Turned out, angels did get car sick. Kind of.

Simon arrived in Atlanta with a new working definition of the word eternity: four hours on a bus with a pissy angel.

Wasn't like Mack could sit in his own seat. Rather a bit too ethereal for that. Simon had been lucky to get on at all, much less get an empty seat next to his.

Mack spent the first hour standing in the aisle, dissipating every time somebody got up to use the toilet. Eventually, he got tired of all the passing-throughs and went up front to sit on the step near the driver.

It was hard to drown out the sound of his complaining. Driver drove too fast. Too slow. Too close to the car in front. Too near to the edge of the road. Wore too much cologne. Fooled with his phone too much. Simon passed most of the ride chuckling into his collar, trying not to draw attention. It was hard to look sane while laughing at a ridiculous creature no one else could see. Little too much Drop Dead Fred.

Mack's indignant tirade almost made the ride bearable...but a bus was still a bus, and he'd gotten on with a rough stomach to begin with.

If only laughter really was the best medicine.

Unfortunately, this malady had a lousy prognosis. It was terminal. Every deal with the Devil ended the same way.

Simon drew a shallow breath, trying not to wake the cramps again.

At least Mack seemed impervious to diesel fumes. Simon, on the other hand, wasn't. The smell left him feeling dizzy and nauseous, a little unsteady on his feet.

Or, maybe it had been the ride itself that left him a wreck. Angel portals were a thrill ride for him, but buses? Reduced the mighty mage to a puddle of sea-green in a wastebasket, every time. Fricken car sick nonsense—

He staggered the corner and leaned heavily against the wall, breathing deep in the ocean of clean, bus-free air. Or, maybe it was his tattoo. It had taken a will of steel to avoid it but he hadn't touched it once on the entire ride north. Maybe he was jonesing for a hit. God only knew how he felt between regular old wand-hits before. Withdrawal was a nauseating bitch.

Or...maybe not. He rubbed his mouth and leaned to spit into the gutter. If it was the tattoo, he'd know it, period. The hold it had on him was bone deep. Soul deep. If he were simply hungering for a wand hit, he'd know it even if he were dead.

Mack had regained his ethereal composure, manifesting enough to allow the soft breeze to stir his clothing, his hair. Peace had once more assumed its natural order upon his countenance.

Kind of a shame, Simon thought. The harried I-hate-buses bus look was way more interesting. Made him feel like they were on equal footing.

Not like that would ever be possible. Not now.

"So, chum." Simon shook off the sense of impending despair and rubbed his hands together. "Give us a map, why don't you?"

Without a word, Mack procured his pouch of angel dust and poured himself a handful, throwing up the glimmering veil of map. A single tap of a pale finger brought forth the lines and curves of street and road, revealing the odd wobbly spider web shape that bulls-eyed the city of Atlanta.

"And us?" Simon glanced from the map to Mack's face and back. "Does this thing zoom in?"

He reached up to expand it with his fingers, knowing his hand would pass right through.

Except, it didn't.

He felt the veil, a cool slip like a benign jellyfish, alive with a pulse of life. The veil clung to him and he spun it thinner, bringing forth new details. His lips parted in a smile as he relished the control, the touch of angel magic, the power.

Until it began to burn.

He snatched his hand away and rubbed his fingertips, soothing away the nips of tingly pain. But the map...

It now bore the brand of a human hand print, a dark scar across the face of the bluish-purple sheen.

Mack stood agape, staring through the damaged veil at Simon.

"I—I'm sorry. I know I shouldn't have—I" Simon stammered, regretting so many things all at once. He had no right to touch it. Didn't even know where the impulse had come from. Just knew that looking wasn't enough. So surprised he'd felt it, the joy, the surge of victory at having done so. And the crush of regret that he'd ruined it, tainted it, marked it with his lowly undeserving mortal flesh. "Did I break it?"

Mack's eyes were dimmed beneath his furrowed brows. He tapped the veil, but it didn't respond to his touch.

"Just great," Simon muttered. It was locked up, or something. The Holy Internet crashed. His fault. Again.

"This is of no use." Mack waved a hand and the chrism veil disintegrated into dull sand, falling to the sidewalk with a soft hiss. "You will need to rely on conventional means. Or, rather as is generally the case with you, unconventional."

If he only knew. Simon nodded, scrubbing at the grains of dead chrism with the toe of one shoe. Only a moment ago it had been bright, and shimmering, and full of wonder. Now, it was now little more than scattered dirt, a chilling reminder of what lay ahead for him and every other foolish mortal who dared to believe that something glorious awaited in the hereafter.

Such pessimism was not to be shared. Exorcists, more than anyone else, had to believe in the Life After. It was the only decent reason to keep risking the life he currently had.

Thing was, before he went through the Devil's portal, he didn't have to work so hard at believing it. "Righto. So. First step first."

Scanning the street, he selected a friendly-looking passerby and strode over to her. A small inquiry made. A smile, a point of a finger, and a thank you.

Returning to Mack, he jerked his head in the direction in which the woman had pointed. "Come on. We go this way."

Behind him, the angel called out. "What did you ask that person?"

He only gestured over his shoulder for Mack to catch up.

Which the angel did, in a moment. Honestly, he moved like he had a Segue under his tunic. Maybe he did. Those pants he wore were pretty loose-fitting. "Simon, what is this 'first step'?"

"The same as every other first step. I found us a Dunkies. Every plan starts with a coffee, Mack." He clapped the angel around the shoulder and steered him in the right direction. "I figured you knew that by now."

Soon thereafter, the pair leaned against a low stone wall on one of the multitude of Peachtree Streets (Simon had trouble keeping track of them all), this particular one a lovely tree-lined sidewalk beside the busy lanes of city traffic. He had to admit, there was a certain charm to this place, a warmth beneath the annoying humid heat of a southern city.

There was another force in this place that attracted him, resonated with him. While he'd always been intrigued by new places, this was more than the change in speech patterns, the difference in pace, or the odd obsession with sweet tea. Atlanta had a sense of Something Big on the Way.

Big cities usually had that feeling about them. It was growth and change and the cumulative desires of tens of thousands of men and women who were all thriving in the heart of urban life, changing and morphing with each breath.

Yet, this place was slightly different. It was the same typical city feeling, but this time, it lay on a deeper, metaphysical level. He closed his eyes and inhaled over his cup of coffee regular, feeling out the ley lines beneath his feet. If he hadn't been so focused on saving one person, he could admit he should have relocated here a long, long time ago.

There was a lot of work here to be done. He didn't need the scrying lens or the damnable Sight to confirm it. So many doors here, waiting to be opened.

Mack seemed nonplussed by the whole change of scenery or the dull ache of foreshadowing that coated it, although he was quieter than usual.

He was staring at Simon. Studying. Scrutinizing. Suspicious. That mess with the chrism veil didn't abate that a single bit.

Well. Let him scrutinize, Simon thought. He had work to do. Always had work to do.

Squinting in the sunlight, Simon shielded his eyes with one hand, slugging down another mouthful of coffee. It would take a while to acclimate to this new city, to absorb the natural energies, the humanity, the residual powers. It was like taring a scale—he had to identify the baseline before he could notice the anomalies.

His tattoo pinched up about then, giving skin crawl a new definition. Dammit. He must have triggered his tat without meaning to do so. This wasn't the time for a distraction. He barely had time to get the Coffee Beast fed. Now the tattoo was looking for attention.

He rubbed it with a frown, annoyed more than anything else. But it was more than an unitchable itch. It was a sense of...*open your eyes, fool.*

Not one to ignore a magical warning, he did as he was told. He opened his eyes and looked, hard, everywhere, at everything, everyone.

When his gaze fell upon a certain man across the street, his senses just locked onto him.

The big burly man stood out amongst the others around him. He didn't look comfortable in his own skin. He walked like his clothes didn't fit, or like he was going commando. Sunlight filtering down through the leaves glinted off his reddish-brown hair as he lumbered away from them, toward the Marietta district. He looked over his shoulder once, in Simon's direction.

Simon's throat closed around a swallow. That face. That was definitely him. The man from his wand-tripping visions.

Silently he followed, moving in lockstep, using trees and poles as camouflage. Couldn't lose him, couldn't spook him. Zeroed in on the guy, Simon patted himself down for his cigarettes and pulled out the pack, tapping it against his palm.

One by one the cigarettes slid out. He picked them free, tossing them to the ground. It wasn't a smoke he wanted. It was chicory. He needed an invisibility spell.

The pack crumpled when the last cigarette fell out. Not a single stick of it. Shit.

So, he did the only other thing he could. In a last ditch effort, he closed his eyes and willed himself not to be seen.

The tattoo hummed and churned out a sheen of magic that slicked over him from head to toe. He knew it worked. No one saw him, not even the guy who shouldered past him, eyes on his phone.

Simon didn't look back to see if Mack followed. Hopefully, he didn't. He didn't want to have to explain what just happened.

The hulking mass of redhead turned west on Baker. Simon glided behind him, unseen. He wanted to snare him, interrogate him, turn him inside out until he gave up everything Simon needed to know. And with the passing of every block, he realized something else: he hated him.

He flat-out loathed, despised, atomic-rage hated him. For no reason. None he could figure, anyway. The feeling just washed over him like a boiling rain, soaking him with seeping hate. By the time they got to the aquarium, he was drowning in the angry red roil.

He reached up to rake back his hair but stopped, startled, just short of burning his face off. His hands were coated in greasy blue flames. Hellfire. He didn't even remember summoning it. Quickly, he rolled his hands beneath his armpits, stifling the flames. Thank God he was more or less invisible.

But, dammit. That little bit of lighting up had cost him. The guy was gone, lost in the traffic.

Simon closed his eyes in despair. Stupid, stupid, stupid. He stood on the corner, trying to look everywhere at once. All this way, only to lose him in a crowd of tourists.

"Simon." Mack pressed a hand to his elbow. "You were difficult to locate. I assume you have located a lead?"

"That was him, Mack. That was the face from my vision. Back in Boston." Simon slumped against the wall, wishing he wanted a smoke, just for something to do with his hands. His hands itched for action but, when the simple act of snapping your fingers made them burst into hellfire, a guy had to look for a different outlet for nervous energy.

Mack peered around, seeking the stranger, eyes narrowed with scrutiny. "There was a presence back there, before you vanished. He was not human."

"That's just fricken great. What is he? A gargoyle? Minotaur?"

"He is an..." Mack's voice trailed off as if he were being gently strangled.

"An?" He prompted him with a rolling-hands gesture.

"Extremely formidable opponent." Mack slid his hands into his pockets.

Simon hadn't even known that angel clothes had pockets.

He'd sort of figured he'd only have leather pouches hanging from his belt, *a la* the nearest Ren faire.

Wait. Did Mack wear a belt? Honestly. Sometimes he doubted the dude even wore shoes, he was so rustic. "So, that's it? You look like you've seen a ghost, or whatever it is that scares the pants off an angel, and all I get is 'extremely formidable opponent'? Why does this scene feel so familiar?"

"Enough foolishness, Simon. This is very grave. I must deliver something unto you."

His eyebrows went up. "Uh, oh. I don't like it when you talk Biblical."

"You must take this." Pulling his hand out of his pocket, Mack held out a small bundle of faded, rough-weave fabric, secured with a thin strand of fraying rope.

"A present? For me?" Simon gave it a scouring look without taking it. "Who gift wrapped it? Medieval Pier 1 Imports?"

"It is a relic."

Oh, was that all? Simon relaxed and let go of the breath he hadn't realized he was holding. "You mean, a charm."

"It is a relic, not a charm."

"You say to-*may*-to, I say to-*mah*-to—"

"I say *relic*." Mack looked grumpy. "And so you shall say, also, if you want this to be effective. It's not just the relic; it is the faith and piety you put into it that makes it powerful."

Simon huffed. Angels could be so hoity-toity sometimes when it came to the divine stuff. "Fine, whatever. Relic. Let me see this great big fricken relic, then."

Mack placed it gently into Simon's open hand like it was a baby. Or an unexploded land mine.

At this point in the game, neither would surprise him. "Do I open it?"

The angel almost gasped. "No! You just—do not unwrap it. It has been preserved in this way for more than a thousand years. Just because humans are temporary they think everything is disposable."

"It looks like something a peasant would have played with, if he could actually afford a dirty rag on a stick."

"Simon." Aghast, Mack's voice dropped to a bruised whisper. "You are holding the blessed remains of a Saint."

All the jokes ran out of him like boggy water from a cooler the day after a tailgate party. Suddenly, he felt like he actually was holding a baby or an unexploded land mine. Quite possibly, a baby playing with an unexploded land mine.

This wasn't just a relic. It was a *Relic* relic. The real deal.

And he knew it was the real deal, because his hand had started to sting, a tight line of pain that went from his palm to his tattoo. An allergic reaction of the unearthly kind.

He stowed the bundle into his inside pocket, hoping that his jacket was enough to keep it from singeing his chest. "You just remember you had this on you or is it a bit of emergency preparedness?"

"You must prepare yourself for the worst. A struggle lies ahead."

"Oh, good. A struggle. Just what I need. Thank God I have you." He shrugged at Mack's disapproving look. "What? Seriously. God sent you here, right? I'm thanking Him."

"It sounds more like your usual sarcastic humor."

"It's called gratitude, Mack."

"Yes. Gratitude. A noble expression, when genuine. I must perform reconnaissance. Do not get into trouble." Mack stepped backwards into the sudden fog of his wings, dissipating on a breeze.

Simon rubbed his arm, which still twinged from his brief contact with the Divine relic. "Sheesh, angels."

Crossing his arms, he settled more comfortably against the building and surveyed the sidewalks once more, looking for the man to reappear. Watching, and waiting.

Things an angel did. Not exactly the standard Simon ever thought he use for self-comparison.

His Sight flickered, occasionally painting shadows over people as they drove by, and he tried unsuccessfully to avoid comparing himself to one angel in particular, one who had Fallen way back at the start of it all.

Watching, and waiting. He was doing it, too, from His place below. The shudders that ran down Simon's body were cold, so cold. So unlike the city that promised something else would burn, and soon.

22

Luminea replaced the crystal stopper and set down the carafe. The light glinted off the exquisite faceting, illuminating the pale amber liquid within. Sometimes, it was satisfying simply to admire the wine.

Sometimes, however, it was necessary to consume it. Tonight was such a night. To use the vulgar vernacular, she needed a stiff drink.

Zophiel had spent the remainder of the day scouting for a new host. She wouldn't have thought it such a trial; Atlanta was a wealthy city. No calloused fishermen or bow-backed farmers here. Men lived easy lives with their computers and luxury office spaces and salons.

What exactly was Zophiel looking for, anyway? How high were his standards?

She lightened a bit. As high as hers. There was no other way. What she wanted was what he wanted. In all things. Until the end.

A new host body would be no different. He would search until he found exactly what she wanted. It was for that reason she did not reprimand him for taking so long to accomplish this task. Good things took time.

Like this wine, she thought, as she gently swirled her glass, the golden vintage shimmying against the sides of the crystal like a tiny tide. Good wine cannot be rushed. Age is its advantage.

Zophiel had politely refused to join her in a nightcap, choosing to remain standing aloof as she lounged upon her settee, gazing out at the twilight that settled over the cityscape. Nightfall was a gentle event in Atlanta, the sun clinging to the skies in the west as if it were reluctant to leave the world behind. Artificial stars twinkled in the forest of tall buildings and the canyons of the streets.

His voice had a quiet contentment when at last he spoke. "Do you remember our first day?"

She smiled and exhaled a bemused laugh through her nose. "I remember Taylor. I had grown fond of the old goose."

"No. Not Taylor. Our first day. When you looked upon me and knew it was me."

This time, she remained quiet. Her gaze froze on the horizon, no longer registering the play of a dying sunset on cold steel. She did remember. She remembered everything…

She woke from the dream in which he appeared to her, gave her detailed instructions on what to do to facilitate his manifestation. He had told Luminea it was he who had appeared as the old fisherman Taylor. It had been he that struck down the drunken brute and rescued her.

He had told her he could do it again—he could take another body, this time one not so frail, not so old. She could chose his next host.

Perhaps Zophiel had meant it as an enticement, a lure to convince her to go along with his plan.

Little had Zophiel known that she had chosen someone, even before she had a plan. All her schemes to consolidate power for herself had been proceeding well and she knew that in order to further her operation, she needed more power, more wealth. She had reached her limits on her own. It was time to expand.

It was time to align herself with a mortal who could provide the materials she needed. And she had just the man in mind.

A frequent visitor to the harbor, Lord Wellton was the aristocrat who collected rents from Bristol's residents. He collected duties and taxes from the ship merchants, royalties from the marketers, rents from the farmers. He had land and wealth and harbor. And, more importantly, he had an unmarried firstborn son.

The young lord was handsome, healthy, and of good cheer. He also had an eye for beautiful women. His gaze had settled upon Luminea many a time but never spared a word. She was not highborn, as he understood the term. She was worth no more than appreciative looks. Only a woman of status would catch his conversation and, subsequently, his hand.

It had been an obstacle to her plan. How would she, an unwed mother, a commoner, a laborer, claim the attention of a human with so elevated a status?

Little had Zophiel known that he would provide her with the key to that locked door.

She had no deliveries to make that day. Instead, she wore her cleanest gown, using Enochian magic to bleach it light and cast a sheen to it, to illuminate the fabric just a little more. She combed and braided her long tresses, wrapping and piling them upon her head with a tumble of ringlets. She had no gown cut from expensive material. She had no tiara of precious metal. But she had beauty, a natural beauty, and she used it to her fullest advantage.

When she went to town, Lord Wellton and his son were at business. Everyone stopped to stare at her. Whispers behind hands. Admiring looks.

And a young lord who stared, agape, amazed to behold such a vision in so rough a town.

She approached the Lord's horses, her gaze set elsewhere, as if her business called. The young lord slid down off his saddle and bowed to her.

"You are in need of an escort, my lady," he called. "Pray, allow me to obtain one for you."

She feigned humility and bowed her head. "Your kindness is much

ASH KRAFTON

appreciated, my lord. May the angels watch over you."

She watched a change shudder through him as he blinked, seeming to wake from a dream. He patted his chest, looked at his hands, rubbed his shoes against the crushed stone before seeking her eyes. "I believe I have already been blessed, for you are a vision of the Divine. I am at your service."

Zophiel had taken him, just as he'd said in her dream. She knew it with absolute certainly. Although she watched him ride away with his "father", she knew she had only to wait until he returned for her.

She had known he was angel inside a stolen human body. She knew it wasn't part of the natural order. It mattered very little. He was someone who understood her, the only being in her world that truly understood her plight. He had begun making daily trips to the harbor, spending hours with her, taking long walks in town and along the shore. Once safely away from the prying ears of the town folk and his disapproving father, she begged him to stay.

Zophiel did as she asked.

He kept the body as a permanent host, assuming the man's life and station. Eventually, he'd overruled his father's wished for a propitious marriage and brought Luminea and her daughter to his purloined country estate. She remembered the grand arrival he'd made in his carriage when he came to collect them. She allowed herself the full glamour of her Enochian power, no longer fearing whispers of witchcraft or devilry.

Her days sewing in a thatched hut in the middle of a filthy wood were over. Her star was rising. Soon, her schemes would advance once more.

And they did, with a meteoric flash.

Outwardly, in face of his family and household, Zophiel played the role of benefactor. To do otherwise would raise suspicions.

Inside, he was above all things an angel. A servant. Now, he simply redirected his service to Luminea.

She'd quickly deduced he was absolutely enthralled with her, and she used it to her advantage. She played him, coerced him, and kept him in check, all the while doling out small favors to keep him satisfied.

Like a puppy.

"Madam?"

His voice startled her. Madam. When exactly did he start using that title? Must have been after they began accumulating staff. He kept order that way, made sure everyone knew who was truly the one in charge.

She alone knew the truth. An Enochian could never best a pure-blooded angel. Enochians were tainted with the weakness of mortality. And she'd been tainted by things far worse than human blood.

But he did not know that. He was as enthralled with her now as he had been right at the beginning. His devotion grew deep strong ensnaring roots. She would always dominate him, in all ways.

She smiled, broadly and sharp. Didn't that just throw a wrench into the Grand Design? She smoothed her expression before turning around.

"I was just remembering, Zophiel. I remember what it was like to finally find safety and security in your embrace."

"Even before, I had watched and protected."

"Yes…but there is a great difference between watching and doing. Speaking of which…" She tapped her lower lip with a slim finger. "There is doing to be done. I think you shall find her awake."

Simon never sleepwalked. Not even as a kid, when he'd done enough dumbness and seen enough horror to have earned sleepwalking privileges for the rest of his life.

He should be asleep in a Hilton, lulled to sleep by the drone of the elevator in the wall next to his room, wondering what Georgians had against sufficient air conditioning.

Yet, here he was, standing at the edge of Chiara's silver pool. Not knowing how he got there, or when, or why. He rubbed his mouth, feeling the stubble of new beard. Most decidedly, there was no good reason he could give as to why because this was the last place he wanted to be.

The surface of the silver water shimmered. He took a wary step back. Not in a hurry to go through that looking glass again.

But the curiosity was so strong, so alluring. No; it was more than curiosity. It was a calling that resonated through him, like the voice of a loved one. That beckoning wasn't an easy thing to ignore, no matter how many alarms were going off.

He leaned over, seeing his reflection in the stillness of the glass-like surface. It shimmered again, blurring his image. When the water stilled, his appearance had changed. Only took a long stupid moment to realize it wasn't his reflection anymore.

It was the Morningstar, eyes gleaming with a hot-white glow.

His voice was more in the head than in the ears. *Luminea plans to damage Chiaroscuro. You must not let that happen.*

Damage. What a weird word. Divinities used the oddest vocabulary. Simon shook his head, trying to focus. Not like this was the time or place for a lazy chat. "How can I stop her? She's Enochian. And she's got a goon that pretty much made my Watcher soil his divine trousers. Safe to say she's not going to be an easy fight."

No. Which is why you need my help.

The water rippled over Lucifer's face and a small object bobbed to the surface, floating. A tiny glass vial, stoppered with a bit of cork, floated over to the edge of the pool, right in front of him.

"Message in a bottle?" Simon plucked it from the water, peering at the object trapped inside the glass.

You know what you must do.

And, just like that, Simon knew. The knowledge was suddenly just there, in his head, like a brick that wouldn't budge.

He knew exactly what he would do and it went against every fiber in his being. His muscles began to tremble as if his electrical had gone haywire. "Why? Why do I have to do it? You have the power, not me."

I cannot travel to your plane.

"You can. You have the pool. I'm sure you didn't go through all that trouble to build a one-way street."

Use your tiny brain, Alliant. What is a pool? A collection of water.

Simon shrugged. "So?"

I am the king of Hell. I command fire. I cannot travel by water.

The Devil's reflection shook violently like a puddle in

Jurassic Park. The surface took on his own appearance as it calmed.

But the voice was still there.

Together, Simon Alliant. The only way.

Bristol
the distant past

Zophiel would not make the same mistake with this body as he had with the old man Taylor.

All that jumping in and out had prematurely aged that first host. At times, he missed his angelic form—missed the flying, the all-seeing, the graces that ran through his being, ready to fall like rain upon the humankind.

He could not abandon this host without fear of destroying another earthly anchor. This human had advantages over the others: money and land and influence.

All the more, Luminea looked keenly at him, smiling in a beguiling way that made his pulse race. She seemed to delight in touching him, simple brushes of a hand, a slight press of her side when they passed close.

She made his body respond in a passionate, ferocious way. Each day, his obsession—his addiction—grew stronger, deeper. All thought of being God's Spy, the angel Zophiel, dimmed and faded when he stood in the luminescence of this enrapturing woman.

He was fallen and he didn't even know it.

Hidden inside a mortal body, concealed by flesh—other angels could not find him. He hid in plain sight of all Creation. While the mortal body allowed him to stand upon the earth, he retained much of his angelic power. He simply did not need it when Luminea was near.

She was the miracle, not he. He was content to be mundane.

He did not realize he'd fallen until many years later, when the young Lord Wellton's mortal body began to fail to the same familial disease that had prematurely—but serendipitously—eliminated his disapproving father. He needed a new host. Together, he and Luminea spent many dark nights, plotting their next move. They took many long trips, surveying the local gentry. They made many secret inquiries, looking for a new location for their power base.

All was done covertly, and with alacrity. Luminea was not aging as humans did. They couldn't stay forever without rousing suspicions.

She was as clever and as shrewd as any war general. Zophiel simultaneously admired and feared her determination. Piece by piece, their plans fell into line. A secluded estate where they could live in privacy. A handsome young man who looked similar to his current host.

Zophiel rode out one evening to complete the transfer and dispatch the discarded lord.

The moon was full and heavy, casting a noonday brightness upon the manor house. Using his angelic Allure, he drew out the next host and stunned him with a moment of Rapture to hold him still.

He wrenched himself free of his host, preparing the transfer. It needed to be done quickly. The loss of mortal sensation made him feel as if he'd been sealed in a crypt. He couldn't breathe—didn't need to, just wanted to—

And just as he readied to descend, as he tucked his wings around him preparing to force his essence into the new mortal host, he saw them.

His wings. Black as a moonless night. The color of the Fallen. He saw them and he knew.

Steeling his resolve, he shoved his way into the new host, taking possession immediately. A simple mental fist around the old host's throat choked the life out of it. All that had remained to do was stripping it down, destroying its face, and leaving it in the woods for animals to discover.

Hurrying back to the manor, he penned a letter to the host's family, informing them that he was off for the north, and packed up a great deal of the family fortune in a carriage before leaving at dawn.

He didn't tell Luminea about his wings. He simply arrived at their home in his new host, spoke their predetermined phrase, and off they went, taking the fortunes of both aristocrats with them. Luminea cast a Sleep upon Chiara and spent the majority of the ride doing very pleasurable things to Zophiel, things he'd never imagined were possible. To reward him, she'd said. To reward them both.

Apparently, this new form pleased her. He filed it away in his mental vault and succumbed to her charms, body and soul.

Thus, he remained in her thrall.

They had an intense relationship. Master and slave, yet intimate in countless ways. Zophiel had been innocent of the ways of a man and woman, Luminea his dutiful tutor. They never fully consummated their relationship but he hadn't realized it until a serving girl proved to be more than just a person to carry trays from room to room. She'd offered her service in a new way and, one afternoon, taught him something quite astonishing.

Human bodies were designed to fit together.

Luminea, of course, could not know about this excursion. He used the girl frequently, usually after Luminea had been with him. The girl gave him a sense of completion Luminea never offered.

He dared not ask why. This knowledge of mortal intimacy had to have been learned somewhere, and he knew the girl would not survive very long once Luminea learned of her tutoring.

When the wench told him she'd conceived his child, he panicked. The girl had gone from treat to threat with a simple statement. He portaled her out, away, gone, not even thinking twice.

It wasn't until much later that he'd considered the ramifications of fathering children on mortals, when decades of living with the strategic Enochian made him realize the practice may have a tactical value.

So, for centuries they continued their intensely personal relationship, one of dominance and submission. Whenever the heat in his blood grew too fierce to leave half-satisfied, he took it out on mortal women. Often, his heated frustration made the encounters dangerous.

He learned some women enjoyed such activity. He didn't care what they enjoyed. He needed to vent his lust in a non-personal way because he only had room in his heart for one being: Luminea. He served her, worshiped her, and loved her.

And Chiara never knew, not any of it.

Zophiel watched the captive pace the length of her suite, over and over, evaluating the woman who had once been his foster daughter. The need for secrecy, the need to masquerade as Enochian had long since passed by. She knew who he was, now.

Once, Chiara's viewpoints on the necessity of balance and interference would have would have resulted in swift action on her part. He would have been at risk for one of her corrections. He'd kept his secrets carefully hidden, knowing discovery would have brought things to an unpleasant end for him.

A smile ghosted across his face. He no longer needed to pretend because she had been contained. The wards blocked out any divine power that did not stem from him or Luminea. Thusly stripped of her advantages, Chiaroscuro remained firmly within her mother's possession, awaiting the fate that had carefully devised.

There was no other outcome to this situation. There would be no correction.

Zophiel thought about the remainder of Chiara's ignorance—of his physical desires, of his tendencies to vent. That she remained unaware was most definitely for the best.

Because if she knew, she'd be much less willing to cooperate. And, sometimes, a little cooperation went a long, long way, especially when it came to the ways of man and woman.

Chiara didn't turn around when the air changed. She knew it was Zophiel. Even if he hadn't admitted he was an angel, she would have known. She could feel it. Her power was severely hampered her in her mother's fortress, but her blood was still her blood.

The touch of his power made the back of her throat clench. "What do you want?"

"To ready you. Your mother's plans advance."

She spared him a glance, noting the garment bag he carried. "My mother's plans require a costume change?"

"She did not send this." He laid the bag over the chair and slowly unzipped it. Pulling the hanger free of the plastic overlay, he removed a silky scarlet garment. "This will look very lovely on you. Red has always been your color."

She did not agree. Red was the color of lust and anger—two qualities she expressed only on rare occasion. But when she did…oh, they were feelings of the reddest shade, and they fit her more closely than she would ever be comfortable to admit.

Zophiel was pushing her closer to one of those emotions now, and no dress, not even one this low-cut and clingy, would be worth the wrath she would bring.

"Why are you doing this?" She yanked the dress from his hands and flung it to the floor, where it lay in a scarlet puddle. With a toss of her hair she sat down, crossing her arms, lifting her chin in her best impression of her mother. "Why are you still here?

"I am loyal." He seemed unaffected by her outburst. "You have never been able to grasp the concept."

"No, I understand why you are with her. I mean, why are you on this plane? You're an angel. If you Fell, you would be…" She let it trail off, unwilling to choose the wrong word. Such was the danger of living on the silver razor's edge, the line between darkness and light.

"Not all angels Fall into darkness." His voice was mild, coy, teasing. "Some just Fall into a dimly lit place and they find a new source of light."

"You have no right to be here," she said. Anger was simmering inside her, waiting for another bump in temperature. This creature was an abomination. There were divine rules even she would not break. Zophiel's treachery went beyond needing correction. It required eradication. "You are not a Watcher. You hijacked a human body."

"And so?"

"You deserve exorcism."

"And just who will do it?" Still calm, still serene, he spoke to her as if she were nothing but a silly child. "You seem to forget you are in a fortress, manned by very loyal hands."

"You are looking at her." She stood and licked her lips. "Your place is—"

He laughed, the first indication of actual emotion, and it was unkind. "Where? Below? No, it isn't. Above? Obviously not. You cannot exorcise me because I have no place else to go."

So. That was the source of his lofty serenity. The unwavering belief that he ran a foolproof plan.

Well. This wouldn't be the first bubble she'd burst. She drew a deep breath and whispered a single, damning word: "Sheol."

He whipped a look at her as if startled by the sound of her voice. As if he hadn't truly known she was there until that moment. "What?"

Too quick, that response. Too quick because it was urged on by alarm. Good. She lowered her voice, settling into a more hypnotic tone, and paced a slow wide circle around him. "You will go to Sheol."

Hot emotion lit his eyes but he said nothing as he followed her path.

"You surrendered your place in Heaven by stealing free will. Your sin has condemned you." She shrugged. "Honestly, I don't know how you did it. Even the Morningstar didn't commandeer true will. Just rebellion. But you—what you did is nothing short of legendary. And it will never be forgotten, not even by the One whose motto is, quite literally, 'forgive and forget'. Banished from Heaven, even if you were to decide to repent and return. They don't want you anymore. If I pull you out of that mortal body...and if Hell doesn't have your name on its roster..." She smiled, thin and menacing. "That only leaves Sheol."

Zophiel clenched his teeth, his jaw bunching. "You would not dare."

"Would I not?" She arched a brow at him.

It drove him deeper into his indignation, making his voice gravelly. "Who are you, that you would dare murder an angel?"

"Oh." She clucked her tongue. "I would never murder. Not an angel, not anyone. That would be...unforgivable. I would only restore a balance. I would right a wrong."

"You would kill this mortal body." He thumped his palms against his chest. "End this life."

"You ended it the minute you stole it." She flexed her fingers, rubbing her hands together. "Your exile to Sheol is deserved."

"Be that as it may. I am firmly beyond the reach of judgment."

He was, was he? Her reach was longer than he suspected. She tugged the tin of chrism out of her pocket and popped it open. She'd stuff it down his throat, if she had to.

Mouth set in a grim line, she quickly scooped out a handful of the sparkling gel and launched herself at him.

He portaled, sidestepping her as if she were a bumbling toddler, and landed a massive blow between her shoulders that sent her crashing into the coffee table.

The chrism slipped out of her fingers, the largest portion slopping onto the carpet, where it melted before her eyes, drunk in by the twisted wards that had once belonged to the Light.

Several globs of the holy salve splashed onto her exposed skin, causing slick stings wherever it landed. Her neck scalded, her cheek burned. Frantically, she scrubbed the chrism away, her fingertips red and raw from prolonged contact with the powerful relic.

Zophiel roughly yanked her to her feet and grabbed her chin, peering at the smear of sparkling wetness a moment. Slowly, deliberately, he licked it off her cheek.

She twisted away but he held her fast. It was lewd and intimate and revolting—

And terrifying. Her greatest weapon, useless, because an angel couldn't be hurt by weapons forged to fight the Darkness.

"No." He laughed and shoved her away, eyes alight with a cruel joy. "There will be no retribution. There will only be me, getting what I want, and you, doing it for me."

She covered her tender cheek, the heat from her hand amplifying the pain. "Which is?"

"Providing your illustrious mother with her most deserved posterity."

"Don't get your hopes up." Straightening, she sniffed,

disdain in every stubborn line of her body. "I won't be starting a family any time soon."

"Perhaps you haven't met the right man. Don't worry." He leered and gave her a lingering up and down look as he sauntered past. "Fate has a funny way of making things work out around here."

"By the way," he said. He paused by the mirror, fingering his hair back into place. "I'm rather thrilled to see you like things rough. It will keep things interesting. How do you feel about...bondage games?"

With a twist of his wrist, he used his power to pull her hands overhead, binding her wrists with an unseen force. A chain manifested from the ceiling, a hook dangling from the end. Gesturing with his fingers again, he secured her bindings to the chain and hoisted her.

She had to go up on tiptoe to maintain contact with the floor.

Smiling his approval, Zophiel winked at her. "You hang out here a while. I'll be back for you, soon enough."

Blowing a kiss to her, he portaled out of sight.

Fighting to breathe, every muscle screaming, Chiara dangled from the chain, very much at the mercy of an angel who had forgotten the face of God.

Simon needed someplace clean.

After the fitful sleep and trip down Devil's Lane, he needed out of the city, out of the noise and the smoke and the pulse of mechanical life. His double sight was doing overtime down here. So many shadows, so many demtrails, as he'd started calling those black strings—it all pulled in in every direction as once. His blood hummed with a constant zip of the other magic, demanding action, leading him to decisions and impulses that were not his own.

He didn't like feeling like he was a remote-controlled toy. He had a mission. He was in charge of this rescue operation. Not him. Lucifer was acting like the world's most annoying back seat driver.

He tried body dousing a few times, just closed his eyes and let his feet do the walking. His magic and his connection to the magicks within the earth usually led him where he needed to go.

Figured like a scientific thing to do. Although he picked several different starting points around town, they always lead to the same block of downtown near the aquarium. And he always arrived in a seriously dangerous mood.

Easy to blame that on the Devil.

So, it was time to go someplace Lucifer didn't want to go. He burned a little chicory, spoke a little spell, and hitched a quick ride east toward Druid Hills. Sounded magic enough on the map. When he arrived, he discovered the ley lines were swollen with potential. Heap big magic.

Just what he liked.

He found a dense, wooded park in the north hills that insulated him from society, from traffic, from sound. It didn't take long for him to erect a stone circle. Nothing grand, like a stone raising; just a simple, earthy ring that drew on the power of the ley and the Druidic tradition he'd learned long ago. Hey, when in Druid Hills, right?

The circle was cool and fresh, like new grass and mountain spring and starlight on a December night. Its energy was serene: a swaying, a hummed chant, a melody that modern man had forgotten how to sing. Stone circles weren't difficult to master, not the construction, anyway. The hard part came after.

The hard part was accepting what the circle wanted to give.

The circle was a *templum*, an observatory. Mages used them to seek, to gain vision. More often than not, the circle made more than a ring, a boundary, a focal point. It required the user to become part of it.

That meant letting go of certain things.

He'd stone-circled before. A great meditation exercise. The perfect excuse to stop beating himself up over something he couldn't fix back then and sure as hell couldn't fix now. Crossing over acted like a big eraser, like the magnetic bar you slid across one of those old iron-shaving drawing board toys. The circle acted like a sieve, just strained out all the parts it didn't want within its ring.

Surveying his works, he slapped his hands on his jeans to

brush them off. It was a good circle. A good place to hide while he got a grip on what he had to do next.

Pretty soon the sun would climb high enough to pierce the tree coverage and bake him right out of his little circle of serenity. Time to cross.

He stepped over the circle, feeling the first tingles before his foot even hit the ground inside. The tingles grew into pricks, the pricks into outright stabs. He felt like he had charged headlong into a briar patch. One foot in, one foot out, his whole body burned—

His first instinct was to get right back out. The circle had other ideas.

One foot was planted firmly within the ring. Rocking backwards with all his weight did nothing. Grunting with exertion, he stopped short of grabbing his thigh with both hands and yanking. No such thing as playing stone circle hokey pokey. Once you started to cross, you crossed all the way. Stones didn't like to be toyed with.

Hesitating on the threshold wouldn't alleviate the pain, either. So only one thing he could really do.

Closing his eyes, gritting his teeth, he crossed over, pushing deeper through the briars, feeling like bleeding to death was a real possibility if this energy took on physical substance.

Suddenly, the circle's border released him and he stumbled into the ring with a nearly-audible pop. Once inside, the sensation faded. But the scenery was drastically changed.

The sun-splattered leafy green forest had disappeared. A protective dome of magic formed a hemisphere that covered the circle, holding back a red-orange haze that pulsed like a bloody fog. The ring of power formed something like a glass hemisphere around him.

The fog seethed, glowing with a sullen pulse. It didn't like being left outside.

He drew a slow steadying breath, looking back at the power the circle had prevented from entering. That was Lucifer out there, or at least the part he'd been lending to him. He glanced down at the bend of his arm, at his tattoo. The outer ring was still there, but it was translucent, as if it had been drained of ink.

In the past, stone circles were a handy way to refresh a soul, sweep offending thought and emotion away, renewing the spirit. Looks like it worked on more than just the mental demons.

He wanted to be grateful. The vice grip in his chest had lessened. He reached into his pocket, feeling for the relic Mack had given him. Touching it didn't hurt. Here in the circle, he was free.

His shoulders crumpled. This was just a circle. He couldn't stay in here forever. Sooner or later he'd have to go out, back into the red fog that waited like a judgement he'd never outrun.

Glancing at the sky, he tried to judge the position of the sun. The reddish haze muddied the sky too much. Never mind. Now was all he had.

"Get to work, boyo," he muttered. "Daylight's burning, somewhere."

He sat down, cross-legged, and closed his eyes. Submerged in the cool press of air and energy, free of distraction from sound or sight, he settled, stage by stage, into a deep meditation. As his nerves quieted and his heart rate slowed, the hunger that never went away became sharper, more pronounced.

Damn circle couldn't fix that bit, could it? The need. The ache that was always with him. It swelled, raised its head and spread its hood like a cobra, as if knowing it was about to be fed.

He slid the wand out and uncapped it. He knew if he opened his eyes, the fog would be boiling, wanting to be part of this disastrous sin.

No. Not sin. He set his jaw. A tool. A device to get a job done.

He started to chant. Didn't need to chant to make it work, but wanted this one to count, wanted this one to make up for all the ones he'd never do again, if only he could get her back. Seemed like he was trying to make a shoddy deal but he didn't care. What was one more?

Didn't even bother trying to line up the wand. Sorta knew he could drop it anywhere and hit the dead center. Like using a large bore needle. At this point, it would be harder to miss.

When the wand hit, it was like he'd driven a spear straight through his arm, impaling himself on the thrust of razor-sharp power. The stars exploded behind his eyes and he threw his head back with a tribal scream.

The magical dome above him took on the drapery of a midnight sky. The stars and their orbits hung precariously overhead. Time bled around him. The ground disappeared. Lightning sizzled through every inch of his body and his vision opened up, opened wide and he saw everything, all at once.

Like a kid in a candy store, he grabbed what he could. Saw the red-headed man, that face he'd first seen in Boston. Felt his otherness, his sameness. Saw the black fist scoop him up, obscuring him.

Behind that face, there were others. Hundreds. But they were all masks. Masks, covering the true being inside. That redhead was just another mask.

He spun around the man's figure, scrutinizing him from all sides. When the sun pivoted and backlit the burly figure, more than simple girth blocked out the sun.

The silhouette had wings.

Real wings. Not foggy shapes like a Watcher.

The man spun and images flowed past him in a hurricane of events, scenes of him doing terrible things to people. Killing men. Abusing women. Getting children on them. And all the while the sun shone down and he basked in the light, the bastard. Basked in the golden rays as if he, for one moment, deserved even a hint of grace. The lecherous murderer.

The sunlight smiled and coalesced into the image of a shining woman, the one in the car, the one who took Chiara. Luminea. The man gazed at her with adoration while he cut and he maimed, all for her.

A fortress snapped into place around them, the wards as plain as text upon a page. It was like he could see it through The

Matrix, lines of code, layers of protection. Just as the circle strained out every last bit of hell power, so did that fortress. That redheaded punk was safely inside with Luminea, the tallies of his sins cascading through the halls like a treacherous river.

The flood of images slowed and came to rest on a lone woman. He saw her. Saw Chiara, her face, her eyes—God, her eyes—

Saw the chain, her arms pulled overhead. Felt her fear. Felt the rage that was closing in on her.

And he knew all, in that moment. Omnipotence. Grabbed what he could, knowing he couldn't keep it all.

The vision broke, shattered when the wand fell from his spasming fingers. Everything in the universe had been there in his head one moment, gone the next. He crumpled over upon himself and slumped to the ground, sprawling on his back, panting.

And when the blood slowed in his ears, he realized he was chanting quietly, repetitively. Metatron's prophesy. *Light's scion, tarnished...*

He replayed the images, describing what he'd seen in a breathless mumble, trying to remember everything he could before it all faded like an opium dream. Only when he felt he'd cemented the necessary memories of his vision did he open his eyes.

The fog was still there, waiting all around him. It wanted him back.

And, now that he had what he needed, he was ready to go back and finish the job.

Standing, he knocked the grass off his clothes and prepared to cross back, grateful he'd built a large enough circle that he didn't bust his head open when he landed. The last thing he needed to do was blood this thing on the way out.

Crossing over didn't hurt nearly as much. He merely stepped out into the fog and it swallowed him whole, squeezing in on him until every last puff was inside. His second vision clicked over once before settling on normal. Nothing of the

Dark here in these woods to hold it.

Just himself, and he was the last thing he wanted to look at.

Back in the city, Simon leaned against the glass window of a bus stop shelter, sunglasses on, coffee in hand, watching down the street for the appearance of his next dreaded ride. It was a little late in the day for sunglasses, and he shouldn't have needed them here in the shade of the cityscape.

However, he'd gotten a look at himself. Better the glasses than have people staring.

Reunited with the dark power, he'd made short work of getting back to the city. All he'd done was stroll out of the woods out to the road. A little snap of his finger, a tiny flick of hellfire, and he was in the front seat of some dude's Jetta. Travelling in style. Sure beat riding in the back of an open pick-up truck. Less bugs.

Guy wouldn't remember a thing, either. When he stopped for gas, Simon slipped out, dropping a tenner on the front seat before strolling away. Dude was too spellbound to know he'd stopped for a hitcher, let alone get a good look at him.

Maybe the guy was a little confused as to why he stopped for gas with a tank more than three-quarters full. The bigger question should have been why he was wearing loafers without socks or why he popped his collar when it obviously wasn't 1991 anymore. But, hey. He wasn't the kind of guy to judge.

He decided to hit the can while he was there. Maybe splash a little cold water on his face, cool his eyes. They were tired and sore from being out in this relentless Southern sun.

But a look in the mirror told him it wasn't sun strain. His eyes were both hemorrhaged, looking like twin balls of blood. Suddenly, retinal cancer seemed like a better deal.

He just leaned on the sink, feeling heavier than he'd ever felt in his life, staring himself in the bloody eyes. *Resignation* was too cheery a word. He couldn't even be upset about it.

At least his nose wasn't bleeding this time.

So. Gas station sunglasses that pinched the soft spots above his ears and hugged his brows like Jordie LaForge's visor. Adjusting the frames, he rubbed the bridge of his nose. Just wasn't his look.

None of this was.

"Simon." Mack's voice startled him. The angel appeared to his left, stepping out of his wing-fog to apparate at his side.

"Hey." He waved weakly, not so much from weariness but rather a sense that he'd done enough to Mack already. Every second that went by felt like he drove a nail in the already-closed door in Heaven's gate, stranding the angel outside with the rest of the unworthy. "Funny meeting you here. Wanna go for another ride?"

"Not in the least." Mack looked positively revolted.

Simon shrugged and swiped at his nose with his thumb. Would be a long, long time before someone got that angel on a bus again. "Well, I kinda need to catch this one so, talk fast."

"We have gone through a rather difficult time as of late, you and I." Mack wore the expression of an apologetic ex who felt bad over the break-up. "My...contact has informed me that the situation has not been mitigated. What I do not need contacts to tell me is that you have made a terrible turning point. That I can see clearly, the dread certainty etched upon your heart."

"Yeah, you can say that. I, uh, had a vision today. You know, the kind you don't approve of. But after years of not having a plan, I got one. Probably a bad one, but it's a plan." Simon paused and took a long chug of his coffee, grateful for the terrible sunglasses. "I know what I have to do."

"I do not like the feel of your aura, Simon. Your plan—I can only assume it's a bad one."

"Oh, the worst." He leaned over and chucked the cup into the trash. "I asked her father for help, and he agreed. I'm going to walk into Luminea's fortress and hell gate him in."

If he'd punched Mack in the holy nads, he couldn't have gotten a more vehement response.

"Are you mad? Have you learned nothing? Allowing a demon to step forth, unhindered? What good can you accomplish by an act that will cause untold damage? A minion against an Enochian—it will just result in another explosion, most likely, but this time, you will be blown to bits."

"Not with this minion. Because he's not a minion. He's..." Simon faltered. Oh, God, he really didn't want to let Mack find out this way. "He's kind of a big deal."

"A big deal?"

"Yeah. Kind of the biggest."

Several long heavy moments trudged by before the illumination of truth hit, the realization of who Chiara's father really was. And Mack just lit right up.

"You must not!" Mack rushed him, grabbed his shirt up in both fists and jacked Simon right up against the wall of the bus shelter. A startled woman yelped and almost dove headfirst into the street. Nose to nose, Mack gritted his teeth, his eyes gleaming with a sallow light. "All this time—I almost cannot believe it, but it is so clear. He's been priming you. To this very end. A hell gate is exactly what He wants. Access to this plane."

"Don't you think I know that? What choice do I have? I can't fight Luminea. I can't beat a divinity, especially not one who is out of her fricken mind. It's hard enough fighting human crazy. I can't begin to imagine divine insanity. And that boy-toy of hers—" The shudders that ran down his back were genuine. "Holy crap, is *he* a mountain of misery. I don't even want to tell you what I think he is—"

"There is no need to tell me. I know what he is. This is a battle you shouldn't fight."

Simon shook himself free of Mack's forceful hold. "What do you mean by that?"

"It's not your place."

"This is my place." Simon spread his hands wide before thumping himself on the chest. "Getting Chiara back is my only place. I was suffocating, Mack, and I didn't even know it. Not until she gave me the air I'd needed. She never gave up on me. I won't give up on her."

"But the adversary is Enochian, Simon. She is of the Light.

To say you are fighting the Light—"

"She's cracked, Mack. She's a bad bulb."

The angel crossed his arms. "Then leave those matters to others. Walk away."

"You know, ever since I met Chiara, you keep telling me to walk away. I'm getting a little sick of it."

"Then obey and I will stop."

Oh, no, he didn't. He did not just tell him to obey. Trigger word, pulled.

The caldera of otherness that constantly simmered in his veins began to boil. A hot voice in the back of his head seethed with indignation.

He was not the one to obey. He was the one to rule. How dare a servant angel, a slave, a mouthpiece dare tell him to obey? A darkness rose from the round up, stilling and chilling him.

"Did you get Sarah back?" Simon stepped into Mack, who stood his ground. "Did you make me face my fears so that I can fix that broken part that kept fucking me up? Did you help me find the closure I needed? Did you make me whole? No. Did God? No. She did. She did all those things. And she is of the Light, too, you bastard. I fight for her. I fight for *her* light. I fight for her because she fights for the rest of us little unworthy men."

Mack stood still as carved stone. The breeze didn't even stir the fabric of his tunic. "Then you fight alone."

Sullenly Simon crossed his arms and leaned back against the frame of the bus stop shelter. "Never asked you to get your feathers dirty."

"No. I mean, you fight alone. Not just without me. Without the Light."

Simon reached up to take off his glasses, like it would help him see Mack more clearly. He barely caught himself in time. "What are you saying?"

"I have my orders. If you insist on doing this, knowing what it will do for the darkness, in full knowledge of that intentional sin..." Mack bowed his head. "I am to withdraw my patronage."

"What, you're leaving me? Abandoning me?" All the fight went out of him, drained out his toes, puddling uselessly at his feet. "You...you can't. I need you more than ever Mack. I need you to hold me together when I do this."

"I have my orders."

"But, Mack." He rolled his lips, sucking hard on them. "This thing will kill me if you aren't there to put me back together when it's over."

"Then you die to bring Lucifer into the world. That is the essence of your sin. All that He does will be on your soul. Is that what you want?"

Simon rolled around the corner of the partition and sank onto the bench, holding his head in in hands. "I just want Chiara back safe."

"Then pray your sacrifice is not in vain."

Simon lifted his chin, staring up at Mack for a long silent moment. He always knew he had a choice, even when others didn't. That was his curse.

He let his gaze drift and jerked his head. "Then you better be off. I don't want you tainted with what I am about to do."

Mack lowered his eyes and nodded once, a resigned sort of sorrow dimming his ephemeral expression.

"Mack. Before you go...I don't let a lot of people in, you know? I work better on my own. Less distraction. Less collateral. If you haven't noticed, I tend to lose the ones I care about. That's the only thing that's perfect about my record." He stood up, wanting to face his sole true companion one last time. "So, I'm not really surprised I have to lose you, too. It's the way of things, right? I just never thought—I mean, I figured an angel would be different—"

He sniffed and rubbed his mouth. Another reason to be thankful for the sunglasses. "I'm sorry. You always had my six. You never did anything but help me. I'm sure I should have been blown to bits by now. And, no, not from that explosion. I mean, from all those minions. The magic. The magic a waste like me doesn't deserve to wield."

Straightening up, he clasped Mack's shoulder. "So, thanks. For all you did. You made me a better man. And I'm sorry that I made life harder you. I'm sorry I let you down."

"It's not me that is disappointed."

"Well." He gritted his teeth. "At least that part is mutual. God helps those who help themselves, right? Well, I guess He's going to have to suck this one up. I'm going to save her. One of us has to do it."

Mack nodded once, then stepped backwards into the fog of his wings, fading from sight.

Alone. Simon was alone.

He palmed his wand. Not for long. And, after that, alone wouldn't matter anymore. The only thing that mattered was her.

From the street, it looked like any modern office building, stretching high above the others, the tallest in the neighborhood. It was a rather new addition, if the cornerstone was accurate. Sleek and sharp, it had been constructed with a slight twist in the frame, giving the sense of a spiral, fluid and lithe and utterly unique against the skyline. For all its grace and beauty, it was still just a building.

Or at least, he hoped it was.

Simon couldn't trust his eyesight anymore. The second Sight that Lucifer's tattoo afforded him was still disorienting and, quite frankly, alarming. All his life, he'd roamed around the planet, knowing he could see what others could not. His magic made him quite unique in that aspect.

He snorted. *Unique* was such a pretty word. Definitely too much so for a ruffian like himself.

But this Sight—this made *unique* sound like it was a

desirable thing. This Sight added a dark layer to everything. Not dim or shadowy dark—just Dark dark. He saw the things that belonged to the Darkness. The pre-manifestation of demon on the brink of possessing. The tethers that Darkness attached to everyone it had touched. All the things he'd never seen before because he wasn't of the Dark.

This wasn't a game. This new tattoo wasn't a magic-shop novelty, a trick learned on the Internet, a nifty spiff of a spell traded between mages in a seedy New York bar long after last call.

He saw these things now because he'd been to Hell. He'd looked the Devil in the eye and asked Him for help. And he'd gotten it. Suddenly, he didn't feel so cocky, all swagger and bravado because he pulled off some flashy mind-bender or a hair-raising exorcism. He felt very small because now he knew just how deep a pile he'd found himself in.

He stared up at the office building like he faced off with the Dark version of Goliath. This—this monstrosity. It was positively dripping with darkness.

And no one could see it but him.

"Dammit, kid," he muttered. "I need you out here to tell me what I'm walking into."

Rubbing his amulet for luck, he set off down the sidewalk, trying (and probably failing) to look inconspicuous. What was the harm in looking like a tourist, head back, gazing at the tall buildings, open-mouthed in admiration?

Besides being mugged, that is. First rule of tourism: never look like a tourist.

Hard not to stare, though. As dark as that building was, it was compelling. He'd never seen anything like this before. And, though it was bad—very, very bad—the student in him was rapt with the new experience.

If he could convince himself that he was justified using this power in the name of science or something, maybe he wouldn't feel so much like every breath led him one less to his ultimate damnation.

He rubbed his face with both hands. There was no justifying what he was doing. Using the Darkness was in itself Darkness, no matter his intent.

So. There would be Hell to pay. May as well get what he needed before they closed the tab.

He'd made it three-quarters the way around the building without seeing as much as a crack, much less a way in. From the ground up—as well as down, he noticed, as his Sight revealed an equally-Dark presence below street level—nothing but solid, oozy, reddish black Dark, with the fattest fricken demtrail he'd ever seen waving from the rooftop like a column of smoke.

As he ran his gaze back down the mirrored side, something caught his eye. A blip in the Sight. A sharp twinge in his arm accompanied a pulse of energy that struck him with a wave of…possessiveness.

His.

That was the gut feeling. Something up there was his, and a sense of fierce, almost dangerous ownership began a slow burn in his chest. *His* and *his* and *his* and how dare anyone build a barrier between himself and what was *his*—

It was an alien idea, something that came from this power, someplace outside. He closed his eyes and leaned back against the low wall in front of the aquarium, letting himself sink into that strange sensation, examining it, looking for something useful.

Ownership was too vague, too rough a description for it. It wasn't just possessiveness…it was sameness. Oneness. Whatever was up there, it wasn't just his. It was part of him. And every stitch of his being wanted it back.

Breathing deep, he let it fill him, let his center give out from under him so he could spin further down, further out. No longer limited to ground underneath and sky overhead, he allowed his energy to find the open space of the sudden, unexpected vision quest. This purloined power gave him a ridiculous level of adeptness and he slipped into quest as easily as if he'd been in ceremony for several days.

What had originally felt like instinct worked and folded itself into vague images. A shape. A silhouette. Sharper. Clearer. A laugh that sounded like Chiara on the verge of an I-told-you-so. Undoubtedly her. A set of feminine curves, a sense of black and white, a feeling of...

...too much. The emotions were thick and convoluted and conflicted as to be nearly indecipherable. These weren't his emotions. These weren't his instincts. Yet he was filled to overflowing with what could only be described, albeit poorly, as familial love, of pride, of guilt, of despair.

And of sheer determination to get her back.

Determination. He opened his eyes and looked to the spot where he'd sensed Chiara. A determination so strong that he almost whited out, his vision going all swimmy and silver. His legs trembled, a shudder going through him.

And behind the shudder, rage.

Nearby a woman cried out. His Sight dimmed, eyes going nearly human-normal. The passersby around him braced themselves against buildings or vehicles, cries of alarm. Murmurs of speculation. The ground shook. Earthquake?

Aw, shit. His stomach dropped. That was no earthquake. That was him.

A new sensation, one of being seen. Looking back to the swollen tick of a probably heavily-guarded fortress, he swallowed hard. Someone else felt those tremors. They knew he was here. No time to lose.

Nothing much left to lose, period.

Swiping the perspiration from his upper lip, he pulled his charm ring out of his pocket and crossed the street, heading directly for the only thing that looked like a front door. Little point to subterfuge at this point.

Reaching for the door, he let slip a slick glaze of hellfire from his fingers. He could just go in, hell guns blazing, and burn his way up to her, destroy everything that dared to stand between them.

A subtler hint of warmth on his chest made him stop. His

amulet.

The one thing that remained untainted. It was all that was left that was truly him. Or, at least, who he used to be.

Palming it, he knew the amulet was untouched by this Darkness, this wicked power that churned his blood like a food chopper. It was still him. Every experience, every master, every fricken life lesson he'd stumbled over along the way—all of it had a purpose. It was all to serve the Light.

Not serve the way angels served, with their unwavering wide-eyed surety. They knew God existed. They'd been in His presence. It was ingrained in their very beings.

He served the Light the way a mortal served, one who'd seen Dark things at a tender age, had made deplorable mistakes, and tried so fricken hard not to balls everything up again, while knowing he would, over and over. He served in a bumbling, inept fashion, as inept as his magic and just as serendipitous. This amulet had been given to him by his mother, had been blooded with every attempt he'd made at becoming better than what he had been, and had saved his sorry ass more than once.

It warmed his skin again. His amulet hadn't given up on him.

He shouldn't give up, either.

With a deep exhale, he mentally pushed the Darkness from his Sight, his skin, himself. He pushed it down, swept it up into a tidy pile and held it fast in a mental fist. He flipped the charm ring in his fingers, identifying and disregarding each one until he found the one he needed, yet had never wanted: the small glass vial, stoppered with cork, that Lucifer had given him.

The vial was the kind teenage girls filled with glitter and wore as pendants, calling it fairy dust.

No glitter in this one. Instead, it held an inch-wide piece of ancient parchment, rolled tightly, upon which the words of a Middle Ages-era binding spell had been penned with minute precision. A textual amulet. Until recently, he'd never even held one, let alone used one. Kent had a book or three in his library that made references to them.

These were amulets of antiquity—very rare, very precious, and very powerful. Simon had figured the woodcut illustrations inside those books were the closest he'd ever get to seeing one.

Until the Devil gave him one.

Without hesitation, he crushed the thin glass ampule between his fingers to free the parchment. The text was tiny, illegible for all that he didn't speak Middle Age anything. Didn't matter. He didn't need to read it.

He popped it into his mouth and swallowed it whole, chanting the release spell, activating the parchment. The magic bloomed like a flower, unfolding itself, opening itself to the sunshine that was Light. Directing that precious power toward the tight mental fist he still clutched tight, he bound the Darkness within with a murmur and a scrap of ancient parchment.

The Sight vanished, the hot voice in the back of his head ceased. All that remained was Simon.

He smiled, cocky and hard, tipping a nod to his reflection in the shiny glass of the door. Yep. It was him, all right.

He pulled open the door, blasted by the bite of air-conditioning, and strode to the elevator, past the unmanned reception desk and the numerous cameras that swiveled to follow his passing.

Time to see what he could do on his own.

28

Luminea stood over the font, watching the images flicker across the surface of the still, golden water. The resolution was so much better than what modern video monitors could provide. She could see every detail of the dark-haired man who dared walk into her property with impunity. "We have company, I believe."

"Not to worry, Madam." Zophiel glanced over. "We are impenetrable."

"Yes. That may be a problem."

"I don't understand."

Luminea stroked the surface, bringing the images closer, zooming in. The man stood in the elevator, staring up at the camera as if he knew she watched. He ruffled his hair and stretched, giving a glimpse of long muscle and lithe limbs.

A sly smile crept across her mouth and her lips parted, the tip of her tongue running over the edges of her teeth. "I want to be penetrable. For that man, there. Come, see, Zophiel."

He stepped closer and looked down into the mirror. Luminea slipped her arms around him from behind, peering over his shoulder. "That body. I want you to have that body."

His voice betrayed his displeasure. "That? He walks into your fortress with no more armor than an old suede jacket. He obviously has no intelligence. Or taste."

"Let him in." She purred against his ear. "Then, let yourself in."

He sighed, a deep breath that made him feel even more barrel-chested than his host body already was. The sudden movement made him shift enough that her cheek brushed his stubbly neck. The sensation, so caustic, so harsh, repelled her and she backed away.

Watching the images of the man in the elevator, she allowed herself to imagine how nice it would be to have a man like that around. So much more her type than this burly ginger of a boulder standing next to her.

Zophiel crossed his arms and lowered his head, looking up at her from under his heavy brows. "Are you sure this is what you want?"

"One thing you need never question is if I know what I want." Her tone was cool. Her heart had grown considerably cooler simply by having to say it.

Zophiel lowered his gaze. His words slid out on edge. "Yes, madam."

She smiled suddenly, and stroked his arm. "Oh, don't be sullen, Zophiel. Change is a good thing."

"I am not sullen. I am only concerned about the appearance of a stranger within the wards of your fortress." He gave the surface of the watching pool the side eye. "That is no ordinary man."

"Yes. But he is still just a man." She resisted looking once more to the stranger in the elevator. He would be here, in the flesh, soon enough. She was patient. "And no match for you. I'm sure you will make short work of it."

She turned her back, allowing him to take his leave. Short work of a minor task, before the great undertakings could finally begin. Surveying the city, she smiled again, looking forward to the pleasantness of a change of scenery.

Simon paced side to side in the elevator. Antsy. He felt antsy.

Part of it was the amulet that was literally sitting in his stomach. The spell felt like a happy cloud in his gut, a pressure somewhere between "hey, I'm here in your belly" and the urgent need to pee. He shifted weight back onto his other foot, trying to ignore it. Pretty sure it wasn't the right time to look for the can.

But this elevator was so damn slow. What, did they have a guy in the basement pulling on a rope, or what?

Only one button was on this panel. It was marked TOP. Pretentious much? Still, one button gave the mistaken impression it would be a quick ride.

Wasn't quick, not by a long shot. Gave him too much time to think. Time to think about the road he took to get here, and the road blocks along the way.

And more than enough time to remember every exorcism

he'd done since he came out of the silver pool. This last stretch of road had been the Devil's Turnpike. Hard to avoid thinking about the toll booth at the end of it all.

But that wasn't what stuck in his mind.

What stuck in his mind was Kent, eternally on replay.

"Simon, give me your amulet..."

The words had hung in the air while Simon's magical life flashed before his eyes. Every master. Every lesson. Every knock-down, every self-punishment. All those years, those memories, those things that dared only to come back in his nightmares, it all came rushing up like a ghost wind to knock the breath out of him. He swallowed around a lump of cotton in his throat and pursed his lips, controlling his breath, trying to slow his thudding pulse.

Kent flicked his gaze from the amulet to Simon's face. "You have a lot of wards on this."

"Yeah, well." He gave his best grimacing grin, the look of one who cared way more than he would ever admit. "It's more or less my merit badge collection."

"How much do you know?"

How did a guy sum up a magical education? Not like he got college credits or kept a resume. "Well, I studied a little Native American medicine, and the rite of Catholic exorcism, and..."

"No. I mean, how much do you know about yourself?"

Simon frowned. "More than I'd like. I'm not exactly a people person. Even I don't like me."

"You seem like a nice enough fellow."

"First rule of magic." Simon folded his hands and squeezed his fingers. "Never trust what you see."

Kent nodded. "But tell me, do you still look with your eyes?"

Ah. Wise old boy, this one. He shook his head. "You don't, either."

"Sir Arthur Conan Doyle once said though Sherlock Holmes: You see but you don't observe. And I do trust what I observe."

"So...?"

"I stopped looking. You don't need your eyes to observe what really matters." Kent tipped his head toward the amulet. "And I don't need to

cast a spell to find out if this is your blooded amulet. I can feel your fear. You put everything you have into this stamped circle of metal. And yet you took it off and you handed it over to me without so much as a protest."

Simon swallowed again but his throat felt stuck shut. Thank God. The last thing he wanted to do was sob in front of this man.

Kent reached across the table and clapped his hand on Simon's arm, urging him to meet his gaze. Simon stubbornly kept his eyes down, holding onto the sight of his amulet.

The old man sighed. "I swear I will not betray your trust. I know you haven't an abundance to share. I will teach you. My wife would kill me if she knew. Lucky for you, we are both safely beyond the reach of her wrath."

Kent took out a handkerchief and scooped up the amulet. "Unless, of course, she took an alternate route through the afterlife. But even if that were the case, I'd have nothing to fear. Alliant the exorcist is here."

When Simon was severed from visual contact with his amulet, he knew his life was in Kent's hands. Literally. Anyone who controlled his blood amulet controlled him, right to the moment of his death and most likely a good deal beyond.

And one thing he knew: Kent was more than familiar with what lay beyond…

Suddenly, the elevator shuddered to a stop, bouncing his lower belly. More than anything, Simon wished Kent stood beside him right now because he had absolutely no idea what would lay beyond.

But he was alone. With a quick prayer to all that was just, he braced himself and watched the doors slide open.

He had a plan. Now, it was time to execute.

Simon stepped out into the empty foyer. It was a high ceilinged, tile-and-marble vault of a room that reminded him of museums. An arched doorway, marble-faced with an intricate gold locking mechanism in the center, stood directly across from him. The floor was paved in polished stone, glinting like quartz, with gilded designs on each one.

Talk about pretentious. He half-expected a god to ride down on a bolt of lightning.

What he didn't expect was a wallop that knocked him forward. He tucked into a roll and bounced back on his feet, finding himself facing off with that burly, barrel-chested man with freckles and wiry red hair.

He straightened up a little. He'd expected a god but this was looking more like a Boston bar fight.

Don't let your guard down, buddy. If this was no more than a drunken brawl, it wouldn't have taken a shit-ton of magic and the Devil's hand to get this far.

Plus, there'd actually be a bar. Glaring omission, right there.

"So," the burly man grumbled. "This is what I must endure for the next handful of decades."

"Excuse me?" Simon flexed his hands, readying his fists.

"I would, if it were possible." The man sighed, a deep sound of great burden. "But it is what my mistress wants."

With a deceptive burst of speed, he thrust forward an open palm. An invisible force slammed into Simon's chest, thumping him back. The amulet warmed, an indignant pulse of heat as it shielded him from the blast.

Though he was protected, he still felt it. Tasted it. He knew what it was.

Angel magic. No wonder Mack couldn't spit it out.

"Funny." Simon snapped his jacket straight and brushed off his sleeve. "I always thought angels were good guys. What the hell is with you?"

"No Hell nor Heaven is with me." The man smiled, crooked bottom teeth showing. "Some are free."

"You mean, none." Simon chuffed out a laugh. "None are free."

"I agree. We all bow to something. I bow to a power so bright, so perfect, that all other sources of Light become shadow, shades of former brilliance. You, on the other hand, bow to me. I have use for you."

"I'm not feeling it." Simon frowned and shook his head. "I don't work with renegade angels."

The man checked himself. "You truly do know my nature."

"Sure. You're a fricken douche bag."

"My true nature," the man spat. "How do you know I am angel?"

"Uh, because number one, you're acting like an obnoxious turd. You sound like an angel, douche bag. And second..."

Simon slid his rings onto his thumbs. They popped with electric blue sparks that zinged along their edges. "I'm in the business of knowing when a divinity is in the wrong body. That guy just doesn't suit you, pal. Totally not your look."

"I agree. Again. Amazing we have such similar ideas. I think it's fate, don't you? We're made for each other."

"Buddy, I can honestly say this—I'll die before I work with you."

"But you mustn't die. Your body must be protected. It is of value. Your mind, however, is no longer necessary."

Lifting his freckled hand, a strange shimmer rolled beneath his skin, a pulse of light. It seemed to reach right for Simon's face.

The light was only a ruse. What hit him was a darkness so massive it dragged Simon under.

The darkness was a torrent of images, memories, every painful moment Simon had ever experienced. The images were 3-D projections, spinning around Simon like the tornado in the Wizard of Oz, except in color and with agony. Ritchie. Sarah. Balazog. Madness. Exorcisms. Bloody eyes. Chiara.

"Oh. Her." The angel's voice pieced the rush of ghosts swirling round Simon, taunting, teasing, torturing. "You failed her, too."

Violent images. Chiara worried, then terrified, then… hanging from her wrists, struggling to breathe, eyes wild with fear.

Then the angel, forcing himself on her.

madness madness madness

Simon screamed, clawing at his eyes, trying to block the barrage of images. Needed—needed a focal point, an anchor— he needed his truest friend.

Mack's face appeared, like a break in the clouds.

It took all the courage he owned to envision Mack. His pale countenance filled Simon with sorrow, knowing how he betrayed the angel by wrecking his alliance with the Light. His intention had been to save a life but, in the process, he'd done terrible things.

Mack's face floated in his focus, dimming the other images. His lips moved, as if speaking. No sound, just the movement of his lips forming a word.

Relic.

Simon blinked. The relic. He saw it in his mind. Grabbed it. Held it in front like a shield. The barrage of images dissipated, all the badness forced back by the power of faith in something good. The world returned, and with it the wretched angel that stared down at him like a predator.

"No…more." Simon clutched his chest, feeling the raging of his heartbeat, gasping for breath.

The treacherous angel smiled, confident, and advanced a pace.

Simon slipped his fingers beneath his jacket, raising his other hand, warding him off. "No more."

"I appreciate your cooperation." The angel reached down and grabbed his collar, pulling him up. "It keeps things cleaner."

Simon used the motion to thrust his hand into his inside pocket, grasping the bundle.

"You think?" With a smile, Simon thrust the bundle up between them, just hoping to land a solid connection. "In the name of the Light, I command thee—"

The ragged bundle made the briefest contact with flesh, and everything just went—

Boom.

A soft, gentle explosion. A burst of expansion and motion. The man crumpled and went down sideways. Smoke-but-not-quite-smoke lingered a moment before it was swept away by a pump of air.

And Simon found himself staring at an actual angel, a figure of translucent pearly glow hovering over him, with the boniest, blackest wings he'd ever seen. The wings were ragged, black feathers sparse, looking like the spokes of a naked umbrella.

Bleak. That was the only way to describe it.

This angel—he wasn't Fallen. He was just…locked out. Heaven was closed to him. The only place for him was Purgatory. And if the stories about angels in Purgatory were true…

Simon swallowed hard. A fight was coming because this guy had nothing left to lose.

How he managed to stay aloft with those wings, Simon had no clue. But one thing he knew, thanks to Mack's tutelage, was that winged angels, no matter the color of the feather, cannot touch the earth.

Cannot was not exactly the right word. *May not* would be more accurate.

The angel fluttered desperately, its damaged wings unable to keep it constantly aloft, and it drifted down. When it touched down, it cried out in pain. Smoke sizzled from its feet, burned. Wrenching away from the ground, it pumped his wretched wings harder. Once, twice, then a lunge—

It spiral-dove straight at Simon, wings tucked tightly to its body, like a divine drill. A last bid to take on a new host.

The amulet warmed again, all the way to screaming hot, and repelled the invasion. When the angel recoiled, Simon reached up and grabbed him, gripping him by the wrist, hanging on with every ounce of strength he possessed.

IMPOSSIBLE! The angel sputtered with outrage. Its voice was cacophony, not meant for human ears. *I CANNOT BE TOUCHED BY MORTAL HANDS!*

"Yeah, well. Today is a day for all sorts of surprises." Simon yanked down and threw his weight onto the angel, body-slamming it to the ground. Pinning it by the throat, he pressed the relic to its forehead. "So, surprise!"

The angel's face froze in an expression of terror, a grey cast creeping over its once-translucent skin. Simon snatched back his hand, releasing it just as the flesh beneath him solidified. He scrambled off and away, watching in curious horror, unwilling to discover what would happen if he maintained contact.

The angel turned to stone, all motion grinding to a stop as if it were cast in super-quick drying cement and then—over.

Scrutinizing the now-still figure, he nudged it with his foot. It was rock, all right.

He glanced at the host, knowing immediately there was

nothing to do for him. The body looked like a discarded larva casing, split in half, a bloody hollow. His had been a tragic, unnecessary loss of life, all because of a greedy angel. The only comfort in it was knowing that this was the last life that angel would take.

Simon spoke a prayer for the dead over the body, hoping that he'd found his peace long ago, that he'd been spared the torment of living with an angel inside him.

As an afterthought, he squatted and used the relic to draw a cross on what remained of the man's forehead, anointing him. It only seemed right to give him the best possible send off.

As for the other "body"...

Simon went back to the stone angel and stood over it. There would be no such anointing.

"I suppose I should say some sort of last words. You were an angel, after all." After a moment of deliberation, he reached down and snapped off one of its fingers, palming it. "Waste not, want not. Amen."

Turning to the door, Simon stood in front of it for a long moment, knowing what lay beyond probably wasn't as easy as exorcising a Lost angel. Hefting the angel's finger, he pressed it to a panel on the door. The locking mechanism slid and whirred and snaked its dead bolts open, purring like a mechanical cat.

Stepping back, Simon tucked the stone finger into his front pocket, waiting. The door shifted and slid open, without even enough time to congratulate himself for his cleverness.

Sunlight poured out of the room beyond, a long slender silhouette stretching from floor to ceiling. He squinted into the glare.

Chiara. Bound. Hanging by her arms.

His view was suddenly obscured by another figure. A woman slid between them, hand on her hip, a smile that only made her eyes look like chips of ice. Cold, sharp, deadly.

"Ah, Zophiel." Luminea walked over to him and kissed him, hard on the mouth, before murmuring breathily against his ear. "It's about time."

"Let's have a look at you." Luminea stepped back from Simon, looking him up and down, appraising, measuring. She pushed his jacket down off his shoulders, letting it drop onto the floor, all the while making tiny appreciative noises.

She was practically salivating. Holy hell. She looked at him like he was a piece of meat. Simon stood absolutely still, following her with his eyes while she continued her assessment.

Which, apparently, included a solid grab on his backside. He resisted the urge to jump forward, out of her reach.

Standing behind him, her breath hot and deep, she rubbed her cheek between his shoulder blades and spooned him. "Oh. I knew it would be worth it."

A protest on his lips, he flicked his eyes over to Chiara. Her eyes looked wide and tight, her lips a thin, desperate line.

His amulet warmed, reminding him it was still there. Smart little bugger. He touched his chest and circled the edge of the pendant through his shirt.

Chiara nodded once, ever so slightly, and blinked a long, hard blink.

She knew it was him. A signal, then. Keep quiet. Play along.

Luminea completed the rear view assessment and stepped in front of him, smoothing his shirt with a lingering touch over his pecs. "Well, Zophiel?"

Well, what? Did she ask something? What did hench-angels say to their bosses? He had no clue. Maybe just agree and play along?

"Yes," he said, flicking his gaze quickly toward Chiara in a bid for help.

Chiara mouthed a word behind Luminea's back.

Simon jiggled his head, not following.

She did it again, more emphatically. Two syllables. Over exaggerated M's at each end.

Oh. Duh. "Madam," he added.

Chiara lowered her eyes just as Luminea turned around.

"Oh, yes, this will do." She ran her palms over his chest, down his sides, lingering near his hips. Turning, she pressed her back up against him, rubbing like a cat against a post. "Am I not a terrific judge of appearance? I knew this was the right body for Zophiel. What do you think, daughter?"

Chiara eyed Simon with something more than suspicion. "I think he's...nice."

"Nice? That's it?" Simon frowned in protest and lifted the bottom of his t-shirt. "Did you see these abs? Obviously, this guy kept fit. Probably ate organic, too. *Nice* is too weak. I was thinking...hot. Yeah. Totally hot."

"Yes." Luminea cast him a side glance. "Well, I'd hoped you would have been a little bit more enthusiastic, Chiaroscuro. After all, you're going to get to know him rather...intimately."

Oh, no. Simon hid a grimace. *Intimately? That can't be good.*

First of all, that woman had just been pawing at him. Didn't take a huge load of brain matter to figure out what definition of *intimate* she was using.

And B, Chiara looked like she'd just swallowed a caterpillar. The kid knew exactly what she'd been getting at and didn't appear to be what a guy would call *happy about it.*

She inhaled, a strained breath between pursed lips. "What are you saying?"

"I told you this was an empire that needed family to run it. You are going to give me that family. I want my progeny. Your father ensured I would never have other children."

Despite the fact that she'd been hung from a hook like a side of beef, Chiara's expression downturned with compassion. Her voice was tiny, apologetic, sympathetic. "He left you…barren?"

"He left me erased." Luminea whipped a look at her daughter, her tone scalding. "Altered. Scarred. Your birth took my womanhood. I am as sexless as an angel. It wasn't enough to leave me bereft and abandoned. He made sure that he would be my last."

The woman stalked around Simon, running her finger across his shoulders, toying with the back of his neck. "Well, Zophiel won't hurt you the way your father hurt me."

"No." Chiara kicked backwards, swinging helplessly from the chain. "You can't do this."

Simon held onto his poker face with every stitch of power he possessed.

"I don't have to do anything," Luminea said. "And, really, neither do you. This one will do all the work and give me what I've wanted for so long. Finally. Children. I cannot remove your father's traits altogether, but it will be well-diluted by pure angel."

"That is a human body, Mother. What you want cannot happen. It is physically impossible."

"Is it? Are you certain? Are you absolutely certain?"

Chiara's face went completely blank. "You mean, you've done this before?"

"Not me, silly. But Zophiel has proven himself to be quite the stud. His children are everywhere. And they possess his qualities, not his donors'. And now, you will bear ours. Mine and his." Luminea took up Simon's hand, entwining it in both her own, and gazed up into his eyes. For a moment, a brightness, an actual warmth lit them, softening the edges of her mouth. It lasted only a moment. "Well, technically, yours and his, but they won't know you. They will only know me. And they will stay with me and they will rule with me and then..."

She shrugged. "I can erase the last remaining stain of His cruelty."

Chiara's voice was little more than a whisper. "Whose cruelty?

"You know damned well whose." Luminea pulled Simon's hand to her mouth, kissing his knuckles. "I will stay right here, with you, my love. I want you to see only my face when you complete this. It will be only me you think of when you seed her."

He tried not to make a face. What was worse, the thought of looking at her or her use of the word "seed"?

Or that she expected him to force himself onto Chiara?

"You should not be here." He did his best arrogant angel impression and shook his head, firmly. "This is an act between a man and a woman. She must be cooperative if she is to...conceive. It's just science."

Luminea looked at him askance.

"It is an act of parents creating children. And I am the mother." She huffed. "Would it be easier if you laid her down? We can chain her to the bed, if you prefer." Luminea thought a few moments in silence, stroking her lower lip with a slender finger. "If I recall, you do prefer that. I will look for the leg irons."

"No, madam," he said hastily. He stepped closer to Chiara, who trembled on her chain so violently that he worried she was going into shock. "This will suffice. If your wish is to watch...Stand back, at the window, so I may see you."

Luminea slid into place, wearing a hungry smile. Shit, this lady was super excited about watching. Something creepy about a chick that was into porn.

"Perhaps, that other window." He jutted his chin at the far side of the room and twisted Chiara around a quarter turn. "There, where I can see all of you, all at once. It will urge me on."

"Please," Chiara whispered, unable to lift her chin to look up at him. Her eyes shone with desperate tears. "Don't do this."

"I must," he murmured. "I have come too far and sacrificed too much to stop now. This will last but a minute."

"My God." She kicked at him, swaying backwards. "You don't actually mean to do this?"

He reached up and caught her wrists, examining her bindings, the hook they draped over. "This will be easier if you cooperate."

Her eyes went wide with unrecognizable terror.

"Keep your arms up," he said, his voice gruff. Using his knee to separate her legs, he dipped and scooped her up by her thighs, planting her around his hips. He'd never touched her like this, not even with the softest of intentions. It was naked and abrasive, the act of holding her becoming an act of abuse. "If you want to survive this, you will so as I command. Up, I said!"

She blinked again, then did as he told, stretching her arms straight overhead. He hoisted her, once, as if to settle her more firmly around his waist.

The loop that held her bindings slipped free of the hook. Her arms sagged down between them and she gasped for breath.

Luminea looked unsure. "Zophiel—"

"You know, madam." Huffing in exasperation, he let Chiara slide to her feet before stepping in front of her. "I can't do this if you're talking. I said, I preferred privacy."

Luminea stalked over to him, evaluating him. "You always did like your toys. Almost as much as I like mine."

Reaching down, she pressed her palm to the front of his jeans and stroked. Her lewd smile faltered.

The angel's finger. He still had it.

She knew he wasn't simply packing a good time.

She pressed her lips into a thin smile and kneed him, hard, dead in the center, missing Zophiel's finger completely.

Paralyzed, he went down with a woof. *Holy fricken...*

The sensation was like a total abdomen cramp and all the wind knocked out of him simultaneously. Kind of transcended pain.

He drooled and rolled over onto his face, and tried to do a systems check. Legs? Still there. Arms? Yep. Lungs? Everything was still there. None of it was happy.

One last thing. He slid a hand beneath him, gingerly scouting his piece. Angel's finger was still intact. Not so sure his balls were. But, he was breathing and at the moment, that was a victory.

"I don't know what you thought by trying to outwit me." Luminea sounded perfectly reasonable, not at all like the worst ball-shattering bitch from hell. "But, as we can see, you're incapable of thought right know. Typical human man. You should really try keeping your brains in your skull."

He rolled onto his side, his knees to his chest, wanting to wrap his hands around her throat. Cupping himself, he lifted his other hand gave her the finger.

She laughed and made a shooing gesture with her fingers.

Looked like a flick. Felt like a bulldozer.

He was swept across the room, hitting a side table with his ribs. The crack sounded too much like bone. The lancing stab in his chest said at least there was nothing wrong with his ears.

The cramping pain was still there, bringing with it the feeling that he was going to vomit and crap his pants, pretty much at the same time. He tried to swallow it down and dragged himself to his feet, sucking air past the pain that seemed to come from everywhere.

But a knee to the balls was a knee to the balls, no matter how tough a guy was. His stomach decided things would be better if he hurled. He leaned and vomited, a thick stream of coffee regular that scratched his throat on the way up.

Wiping his eyes, listening to Luminea's laughter ricochet through his skull, another sensation started, dwarfing the pain, the cramp, the pressure. It was a weirdly familiar sensation. It felt like…red fog.

There, in the puddle at his feet, lay the delicate parchment. The textual amulet.

The binding spell had been broken. The sensation that filled him wasn't pain.

It was power.

He looked up at her through a glare that briefly glazed everything with a glint of silver. Things were going to get good and ugly, now.

32

"You just don't give up, do you, human?" Luminea stood between him and Chiara, her arms crossed. "I must say, it would have been very nice to have your body, your stamina, and your imagination at my behest."

Simon rolled his shoulders and stood upright, surveying the room, watching Luminea slink back to circle her daughter. The pain had been banished completely, replaced by the Darkness. Another damnable bonus. He should have been in for an afternoon on the couch with a heating pad. Or an ice pack. Didn't matter, not after a knee in the balls. Point was: he should have been down for the count.

But not this guy, not with this power. It would take more than testicular obliteration to make him stand down. "You will release her and you will never contact her again."

"What is she to you but an oddity, a uniqueness in a pretty wrapper?" Luminea stroked Chiara's tear-streaked face. "She's all you will never be and you can't stand that. You can't stand knowing she's so much better than you."

"That's not true. Sure, she's better but—"

Luminea's eyes were so fierce they could have thrown sparks. "So you do the only thing you know how and you steal her and you seduce her and to try to learn her secrets and when you've gotten all you wanted you break her so not even she can have herself—"

"No! I am not Him!" Simon roared, knowing that, at this particular moment, it was a little bit of a lie. The binding spell disabled, Lucifer's power was seeping back into his blood, bringing with it an intimate knowledge of who Luminea was and what she had been. But that wasn't all.

Simon also got a touch of Lucifer. Of His unique perspective. Of His role in what Luminea had become. It was a difficult cocktail to swallow. It resonated with a place in his deepest vaults, one he didn't like to remember was even there. Too many skeletons rattling in that closet.

The flash of anger and authority eased back somewhat, allowing Simon to breathe, to process the situation, the external influence, the stark realization of what—of who—he was facing. His words came from a mixture of all that. Some of them his. Some of them...not.

"I get it, love." He marched over to grabbed Luminea by the hand, softening his touch when he realized it was still too gruff. "I see this great wall of hate you hide behind. I know why you built it. I understand. It looks like a fortress that hides an army but it's just a wall, hiding yourself."

She pulled free of his grasp and retreated to the corner of the room.

He let her go, but caught her reflection in the large mirror. Her eyes were thawing beneath an unwilling vulnerability. "A woman. A mother. A heart that had been trampled. It's important to protect yourself and the one you love. Especially when you feel defeated and vulnerable. It's self-preservation. Key to survival. But sometimes you put all your effort and energy into keeping others out and you just end up trapping yourself."

She turned to him, the sunlight catching the edges of her hair and illuminating her face. Her beauty was ethereal, so bright and radiant. It was a face that would give hope to even the lowest sinner, a view of redemption, something higher than himself. He saw that terrible beauty, and the part that wasn't him wanted to reach up, cup it, catch it in his hands like sunlight.

"I have no place to go." She shook her head gently, her voice sounding far away. "This plane is all I have left. What He did to me ruined me. I can't go home. I don't even remember how to get there."

Sensing a shift in the dynamic, Simon went to her and reached once more for her hand. She needed to be held, to be protected from her corrosive outburst. "You were a victim once. You don't have to be one anymore."

"I'm not a victim. I have power. I have leverage. I have a legion. I am no victim."

"Well, she shouldn't be one, either." Simon nodded toward Chiara. "I can't tell you what to do about—Him. But don't make the child pay for it."

"I never hurt her. I am her mother. She is the only good part of anything I ever was. She is all that's good in me." She patted his hand before stepping away from him. The chill had settled onto her again, a brittle, sharp change in the atmosphere. "That's why I have to do this. I can't allow a weakness to remain."

Plunging her hand into the mirror, she pulled out a wicked-looking blade.

Simon bared his teeth, a bull ready to charge. Smoke curled from the corners of his mouth. "You can't conquer the darkness by murdering the Light."

Luminea matched his vicious look with one of her own. "It's called fighting fire with fire, mortal. I'll beat Him at his own game."

"No, I'm sorry. You'll never even come close to beating Him. And if you think you'll start by hurting her, well." Simon stood his ground in front of Chiara, doing his best to shield her. "You'll have to go through me, first."

He snapped out his hands, fingers curled around tongues of blue hellfire.

Luminea smiled a smile that could have cut glass. "Don't threaten me with a good time."

"Simon, no." Chiara drooped her head against his back. "You don't know what she's capable of doing."

Not willing to take his eyes off the Enochian, Simon only craned his neck. "Doesn't matter. I didn't come this far to stand here and let her hurt you."

"You won't be standing long, mortal. The first thing I'm going to do is geld you." Luminea stalked toward them, raising the blade, murmuring words he couldn't decipher. The knife glowed, a mix of silver and gold.

Chiara gasped, a swift sound of pain, and crumpled against him.

He leaned back against her, just a moment, as close to a hug goodbye as the circumstances would allow. "Kid, you run. Run and don't look back."

Simon shook his wrist, and his wand slipped free, dropping down into his fingers.

Chiara groaned. "Your magic isn't enough."

Wasn't it? Already that magic rolled beneath the surface of his skin, as if he'd summoned a storm just by thinking of it. It rolled and built and waited for his command. It was more than his magic—it was Lucifer's, too. The Morningstar. The mother of all storm bringers.

His mouth, though…that was still his. "Would 'I have a trick up my sleeve' sound trite?"

Luminea lifted her hands, her chants growing louder, the knife glowing. Something about the light hurt his eyes, made his skin crawl. She stomped the last few paces toward them.

Simon lifted his left arm, warding off her advance, and

raised his wand.

Luminea laughed and shook her head at him. "Oh, that's so tough."

"It's all I got." He shrugged and rolled his shoulders.

She raised her hand and twisted her wrist, light glinting off the knife. "And it's not enough."

"Isn't it?" He winked at her and jammed the wand into his elbow. The tattoo lit, the silver ring zipped around. His throat burned with his screaming and he just couldn't hear it, so great was the roar in his head.

The overhead lights wavered and cracked. The air pressure went from breathable to cement at the center of a black hole. The windows blew in, glass pulverized and showering them with fragments like sand. A silver line zigzagged down from ceiling to floor, a lingering streak of lightning.

A portal opened. A hell gate.

It split, widening, spreading. Lucifer stepped through, looked around, and tugged his sleeves straight.

"You! How dare you—" Luminea's face crumpled into a mask of loathing. "How did you—?"

"Nice place." Lucifer sniffed, a superior dismissal. "Although I can't say I like the wards. Quite offensive."

"Get out." Her lips curled back, baring teeth. "I banish you."

"You can't banish me. I'm insidious." He stalked toward her, a panther on the prowl. "And truly, that has been the root of the problem all these years. You resent me and you hate yourself because you loved me."

She held the knife between them, keeping him at bay. "I don't love you, rapist."

"No, I'm not a rapist." He glanced at the knife before dismissing it. "I hurt you...but not like that."

"You seduced me because you wanted offspring. Another soldier."

"And you aren't planning to do exactly the same thing? To our daughter?" Lucifer took a deep breath, seeming to quell the rage that had leaked into His voice. "I fell for a woman who was everything I could not be. She was courageous and willing to step beyond that boundaries of safety and familiarity to follow her heart, her passion. *You* seduced *me*. We didn't spend long together, no. I left sooner than you wanted me to."

Luminea curled her hand into a fist, the fingers holding the knife going white with the exertion. She rocked back on her heels and turned away from him. "It's called abandonment."

"I had to leave." Lucifer spread His hands in a small show of apology behind her back. "It was business."

"*I* was business." Her voice quivered, the words betraying her deepest hurt.

"You were a blessing." Since she would not face Him, He placed a tender hand upon her shoulder and turned her toward Him. "A relief. A balm to the constant burn on my soul. You, a scion of the Light. You made me remember what I most mourned. But I tarnished you."

Those words. Simon blinked. The Metatron's prophesy. Which meant...

Luminea keened softly. Her eyes shone with sudden tears. "You could have stayed with me. In paradise."

"Paradise is not meant for me." It was His turn to look away. "I will always be denied that."

She pressed a fist to her mouth, stifling a sob. Luminea's mournful cry cut through to Simon and he saw her for what she really was: a woman, scorned, soured on love because she could not make that one love stay with her. Love became a curse, not just her love for Him—her total capacity for it had been twisted. Love lost its true definition because it had failed her.

And the wounds were still deep, and fresh, and capable of causing pain. Renewed, that pain reduced her to the agony she'd never moved past—only buried beneath guises of scorn and ambition and revenge. She was a woman who needed more comfort than the entire universe would be able to muster.

"You could have loved me," she whispered, daring to touch His face, a hesitant contact.

"I cannot love you." His voice was steel, His gaze direct, His jaw set. "It is a commodity I am not afforded. But I never meant to hurt you."

She nodded, disappointment and disdain trembling her chin. Her walls slid back up. "Cruelty. That is all you know."

"You think the king of Hell has no feelings?" He leaned in toward her, pointing his thumb into his chest. "You forget— Hell was created to punish *me*. I feel it all too well. I am Hell. I am every ounce of pain that Hell has ever tasted."

"You deserve to feel it," she spat.

"That's what I hear." Lucifer took a stiff breath through His nose. "But, see, Luminea, I don't allow my pain to cloud my judgment. I use it. It is my compass, my drive, my fuel. I use it to get the job done."

"As do I." She glanced down at her hands. The knife. She lifted it, and it burned once more with a painful glow. Both Simon and Lucifer winced at the light, simultaneously. "Now step aside and let me finish this task."

"It's already over." Lucifer shook His head ever so slowly. "All of it. Over, now."

"No. Not until she is gone—you love her and I will take that from you." She lunged past Lucifer, who didn't even move to stop her.

All Simon could do was spread his arms and try to shield Chiara. He anticipated a terrible impact, the slice, the rip, the pain of a divine retribution.

Lucifer's voice was sharper than any blade.

"I said: it's over." He held up a hand, pausing her, and twisted His wrist before swiping left. Another portal opened and swallowed her. A silent flash of light.

Luminea was gone.

A strangled cry from behind reminded Simon to look for Chiara. Her eyes were only upon her father.

"What did you do to her?" Her wrists still bound, she grabbed her father's hand. "Was that a hell gate?"

He cupped his daughter's cheek, briefly. His voice was

gentle, full of tender regard. "I sent her home."

"She couldn't go home." Chiara shook him, as if trying to shake sense into him. "That's why she was here, stuck here, where she wasn't happy. She wasn't allowed to go home."

"Because she so decreed, not they." He freed His hand from her nagging grip and tugged His sleeve back into place. "She is Enochian. She belongs there. And now, she will never leave."

"She's really gone?" She searched first his face, then the room. Her voice tiny, she seemed to have forgotten the peril she'd been in so short a time ago. "I didn't get to say…"

"Say what, Chiaroscuro?" Lucifer seemed to regain His usual tone of arrogance. "*Goodbye? I love you?* She meant to torture and kill you."

"But… she's my mother. She raised me. She was all I knew as a child."

"And was she the same woman now? Hate ruined her. Hate for me. I ruined her. I never meant to do it, you know. She was the Light. She was—" His voice trailed off. "But it is settled."

"No." Chiara reached for Him again. "Father. Please. Let me—"

"It is settled." Lucifer's eyes flashed silver and thunder rolled.

Simon tried very hard to look invisible. This time, the magic didn't respond.

Lucifer used a finger to draw a vertical silver line in the air. The shining silver slice opened once more, this once smoother, more elegant, almost breathtaking to behold. A hell gate supreme. Simon drank in the sight, feeling the resonance.

Another gesture, a softer one, and Chiara's bindings fell free, hitting the floor with a metallic *thunk*. He dipped His chin in one last nod to her. "Be well, Daughter."

Lucifer flicked His gaze at Simon before stepping through the portal. It shut behind Him with a metallic zip.

The Devil had left the building.

The silence He left behind was utterly deafening.

"That's it." Simon breathed in, as deep as his bruised side would allow. Poultice time, for sure. And tape. He'd definitely be taping ribs later. "Well. I can't believe I'm still alive."

Hugging his chest, he rubbed his arms against stubborn goosebumps. This is why skyscrapers didn't have window screens. Altitudes meant cold.

An afterthought crept in on kitty cat feet. The tattoo was quiet, cool, unnoticeable. The open drain inside his head was sealed shut. The hell gate was closed, the power dissipated. Right as rain.

This room, on the other hand, looked like a fricken bomb had gone off.

And the kid—he leaked out a low whistle as he took in the sight of her. Chiara looked like she'd been rode hard and put up wet. Her clothing, rumpled, her hair a tangled mess. A severe welt on her cheek, wrists rubbed raw from where they'd tied her. Dark bruises under her eyes, shoulders slumped in weariness. She needed a nap, a bath, and a fifth of Scotch, all simultaneously.

"Let's beat it. I hate Atlanta." He brushed off his jeans and did a quick inventory. Wand, wallet, ring of charms…

Turning away slightly, he surreptitiously cupped himself. Jewels were still there, intact. He closed his eyes and breathed a sigh of relief. Enochian bitch and her stupid threats. "All present and accounted for. You ready?"

When Chiara made no reply, he turned back to look at her.

Chiara's eyes were wide, disbelief etched in every line of her face, and she shook her head slowly, like she didn't recognize him. Once more, the Devil's voice echoed through his head, but it was more memory rather than direct communication. *Light's scion…tarnished.*

Luminea was Love's betrayer. She was the subject of that warning, not Chiara, as Mack had led him to believe. Which meant…the second part of the prophesy—*a crushing blow will deliver to the lone-heart, the mortal savior of souls*—could still refer to himself. He resisted the urge to cup himself again, remembering the crushing blow she actually had delivered.

But he knew better. Chiara was the victim. Just looking at the bewildered hurt of her expression convinced him.

She looked absolutely shell-shocked. What had she been through before he arrived? Far worse than he, certainly, and he felt like his pieces were barely glued together.

"It's okay, kid. You're safe again." He reached for her, needing to feel her warm and alive and real beneath his palms. Needed to know it was over and they were both alive. And free.

She backed away with a jerk of her shoulder.

"What's wrong?" A though hit him low in the gut, fury bubbling up like hot tar as he remembered the mind-storm the renegade angel had forced into his head. His voice slid into an oily dangerous tone, more growl than words. "Did they hurt you?"

"No. They—Simon. What did you do?"

He probably looked like a fish, bulgy-eyed and gaping. "Me? What do you mean?"

"That was my father."

Her voice broke on the last word, as painful to hear as it must have been to say it. Where fury had taken root, a gripping heartbreak froze over, cracking the surface with sharp grief.

Simon had only wanted to save her, single-minded and narrow-visioned and absolutely determined to succeed or die trying. Even then, death was going to end up a long shot because there were a lot of ways to almost die but not quite. If there were two cells left in his body with a heartbeat between them, he'd use them to fight.

That fight, he won. A fistful of charms, a hand full of aces, and a deal with the Devil. If that wasn't a recipe for disaster then one didn't exist.

But he'd emerged victorious. He conquered. He won.

So why did it feel exactly the opposite? Why did she look at him like *he* was the bad guy?

He hung his head, his brain too loud with an unexpected discord. Because he *was* the bad guy. A lifetime of trying to make up for it didn't change the truth, especially when all he did was prove he'd make a bad choice all over again.

A moment of self-blame was all he allowed. It was an indulgence he couldn't afford. If he had to do this all over again...if that was the only way to get Chiara back...the bad choice would still be the choice he made. Results mattered.

"Yeah." He lifted his chin with a cocky tilt. "That was."

"He knew you."

What could he do, but shrug his agreement? "He knows everyone."

"No. He knows you. He's touched you."

"Ah, nope." The way she said it—it was distasteful, like she'd caught them playing Two Minutes in the Closet. "Fricken no, sir, He didn't."

"Simon." She regained her composure, straightened up, and walked over to him. She grabbed his t-shirt by the collar and jerked it back over his shoulder. "New tattoo?"

"Huh?" He twisted his neck to look. Thick black lines streaked over the top of his shoulder. Yanking his shirt over his head, he went to the mirror. Looked like a black hand print, like someone clapped him on the shoulder. "What the hell?"

"Exactly." Chiara took his shirt from his slackened grip and folded it over her arm. "I'm sorry. It's my fault you got caught up in all this."

"How is this your fault? I knew what I was doing when I went looking for Him. I couldn't do it alone. I had to—" He swallowed a thick lump of shame. "I couldn't do it myself. I failed. Again and again and in so many ways. I needed help. I was desperate."

"And He owns you, now. Do you realize what that means? You were the only one—" She covered her mouth and blinked, looking like she just found out the Mayans had miscalculated and the world would end tomorrow. "I mean, you were for the Light. No matter how you talked or acted or pretended. You were for the Light. And now, you can't be. What did I do? What have I done?"

"You didn't do anything." Suddenly, he felt exposed, bare and grotesque in her sight. Taking the shirt from her unresisting hands, he pulled it back on, ashamed of the mark. "I'm the one who got here. And, you know what? I was meant to be here. Mack said the Metatron prophesied this. You were going to be killed by her hand and I stopped it. So knock off with the self-blame. Destiny brought me here. You didn't drag me."

"Didn't I? Curiosity is your downfall, Simon. I know you. 'Look at the odd divinity,' you thought, 'with her lofty heritage. What a hot, delightful mess. Let's see if we can't have us a war.' You know it to be true. And it's my fault she hurt you and it's my fault He marked you."

"None of this is your fault. None of it. Not her, not Him. None of that is your fault."

She bit her lip and turned her head with an angry shake, but not before he saw the slick glimmer in her eyes. That was it, wasn't it? Not the metaphysical battle. Not the fight he gave to get her back.

It was the *her* and the *Him* and the *they*. Poor kid punished herself over her parents' failed paradise. Still, after all these years, God only knew how many. On the inside, she really was still just a kid.

He knew all too well how hard it was to live with that inner child stepping on a person's soul.

He pulled her into his arms and cupped her head against his chest, rocking gently. "It's their fault. Only theirs."

She didn't reply. The slight shudder of her body against him spoke for her. She didn't weep, or wail, or sob; she held tightly to those sounds with the strength he'd come to admire. Actual words would only get lost in a flood.

He held her as long as she allowed him. No need to let go. No need to run. Just one moment, a feeling of solid, dry land beneath their feet before the tides rose again, and they'd be back to treading the water.

Simon wrapped a protective arm around Chiara and led her from her former prison.

He steered her carefully through the debris-littered foyer, where scorched feathers lay in crumbling heaps. The murdered host lay off to one side, the stone carcass of an angel to the other. Try as he did to shield her from those terrible sights, she saw them.

She said nothing.

The elevator was open, expectant. The ride seemed a lot shorter going down than it had going up. Retrospect did that, sometimes.

What kind of mess would the authorities find when they got here? More bodies? More signs of apocalypse? That nose-stinging smell the hell gate had left behind?

The police would probably think it had been a gas leak. An explosion. How convenient. He huffed out a sardonic laugh.

Then again, it always was.

Twilight was taking hold of the city as they walked outside. Night would rise up rapidly now that the sun had fallen. A shiny red car stood parked on the sidewalk in front of the door, the building's entry lights glinting off the glass like a tiger's smile.

He knew the car was his. Back there in the elevator, he had vaguely thought about what they'd do once they'd walked outside. Not like he was keen on buses and a taxi was probably a little on the pricey side. A car. He needed—he *wanted*—a car.

And *viola*, a car was at the curb. The keys would be in the ignition and the tank would be full. It would be because he willed it to be. And no charm in his pocket could have pulled that little trick off.

The bend of his arm thumped with a pulse of swollen satisfaction at the sight of it.

This power. He rolled his lips inward and bit down, hard. This power was so damned easy to use. And the high that went with it—it sizzled through his blood like a shot of seltzer, making him tingly all over. Full of energy, of motion, of being two ticks from a kinetic kaboom.

With a whoop, he took off at a run, hopped onto the hood, and slid across to the driver's side like an action movie hero.

"Simon." By the tone of her voice, Chiara obviously did not share his enthusiasm. She dragged herself to the curb, her hand on the car door, not getting in. She spoke to the ground, unwilling to look at him. "You killed an angel."

"I facilitated his demise." He lifted his finger in protest, emphasizing the fine point. "That's different."

"Yet, the angel is destroyed. It should not have been you."

How could she possibly sound so disappointed? It had been a battle, a righteous one. An exorcism. It was what he did. It was the cornerstone of his continued existence on this planet. It was sanctioned by the Light, too, because he'd had divine assistance.

Technically, anyway. "He said he was going to do things to you. She confirmed it—"

"So, what?" She looked at him now, a look of heat and scorn that burned him. "You destroy a divinity? You're a mortal, Simon. There will be repercussions. This is a game of staggered stakes. There is no eye for an eye here. You destroyed a piece of the Divine."

"He was not divine." The heat was in his voice, too, now. "He was a snake, a black-winged dickbag—"

"That had been a divinity." She shook her head. "You can't just wave a wand and make it go away. Not to mention the elephant in the room."

He grumbled an exaggerated complaint. "Now I'm killing elephants, too?"

"A hell gate. You opened a hell gate, here. On Earth. And you allowed Him to come through." She shook her head. "These are marks that can't be erased. That hand on your shoulder. That ring around your tattoo. That black string that's tied to your soul—"

"You can see that?" He rubbed his mouth, fighting the urge to reach over his shoulders and scratch. "Oh, shit. I know you can. You saw it the minute I walked in, didn't you?"

She nodded, misery pooling in her eyes like tears.

All the fight went out of him, that cocky full-of-hot-air attitude that kept him aloft. He sagged and leaned up against the car. "So, what's it all mean? Am I damned? For good, this time?"

"I don't know, Simon." She shook her tousled head, glancing away as if the answer stood a piece-ways off. "Some things you can't unsee. Some things you can't untouch. Some things are forever."

She blinked rapidly and set her jaw in a stubborn line before meeting his gaze again. "No. We will not be pessimistic. We will go home, and I'll talk to Him. I'll work something out."

"Like a trade?" He barked a laugh. "A bag of your best marbles and a pack of gum in exchange for a mortal's soul? I have the feeling your dad doesn't give things up without a fight."

"No. But there must be something." She straightened herself, giving him a very Chiara-like look. "I am a Daughter of Hell. And I am my mother's child. I'll find something I can use. I am resourceful, and I am persuasive, and..."

She ran her fingers through her hair, her fingers catching in the tangled ends. Pulling open the door, she jerked her head at him to do the same. "I really need a bath. Let's just go home."

Simon flipped down the sun visor and felt along its surface. Nothing but the vanity mirror. Dammit. No CD sleeve and he hadn't even thought about getting a satellite radio subscription. Scanning the channels once more and getting nothing but static, he switched it off with a grunt. This was proving to be a long, terrible drive.

Georgia to Baltimore. Nine hours, straight through. A stick of chicory and a determined whisper to avoid the green stamps. Hammer lane all the way.

At first, he distracted himself by using the power to ease off the pain of his broken ribs. The seat belt had been simply too much to take and Chiara wasn't letting him drive off without wearing it. All he'd wanted was a Vicodin's worth of relief, that was all. But when he felt bones snap into alignment, leaving him absolutely pain-free, he realized the power was more than a metaphysical Vicodin.

It was methadone. And methadone was heroin's best friend.

Definitely not the sort of company an addict should keep.

Entire states passed in a midnight blur of headlight streaks and overhead signs. Chiara slept just about the whole ride. He glanced over frequently to make sure she rested comfortably. Poor kid. What had they done to her? She looked like she'd been through hell.

So had he. No telling if Hell was through with him.

Still. All things considered, it was good to have her back, rumpled mess or no. He thought again of the prophesy he'd more or less prevented. The lone-heart, the mortal savior of souls, was her. Not him. Kind of a relief, that. Not because it put any sort of divine pressure on him, since he couldn't *not* be an exorcist. Rather, it relieved him of an unspoken worry that had gradually seeped in over the last few weeks, since day-tripping to Hell.

While he'd never once considered Chiara to be the threat, he was 99% convinced the prophesy was about Lucifer.

He couldn't bring himself to admit it but he was very worried that the Devil would bring about his demise. His death, his inability to continue doing what he'd always done—any of it. Anything of his the Devil might have ended would have been bad, bad, bad.

Not only was that particular worry abated now, there was also the blessing of knowing that she was the mortal savior all along. Which meant...she could keep up the good fight. She would not be ended. He knew all along she was the important one. Anything that happened to him would not lose the battle for her.

And that was what he'd been worried about the most, even more so than a one-way ticket to the Devil's den. He was afraid his deal, his situation, would screw up everything she'd fought so hard to do. There was no telling what he was in for, now that he was the Devil's pawn. But, at least, she would carry on.

By the time he reached North Carolina, he'd fallen deep

into driving hypnosis. Normally road trips were coffee and cig-fueled journeys with occasional nitro bursts of road rage and frequent gas stops because the Astro simply wasn't big on fuel economy. But not this time.

The car they drove was some kind of Kia electric that got about a bazillion MPG. It must have been one of Luminea's because it smelled like her. Light perfume, some kind of fruit, a little bit of a pheromone. He had to admit—the bitch was wicked, but she smelled like a fresh stripper. And there was never anything wrong with that.

It was telling that someone who was technically a divinity was so eco-minded. Enough to knock the stoutest Republican on his arse.

He drove tunnel-visioned with determination, absolutely intent on getting Chiara back to her safe place. Whenever he tired the least bit he'd absentmindedly scratch his shoulder, let his fingers drag down lightly over the bend of his arm. That was enough. The tattoo did the rest.

The energy just came to him, giving him back his alertness and resolve. It did anything he needed. Dammit if he didn't see the gas gauge bounce up an eighth of a tank at one point.

No wand. Just him. Just a thought, a press of desire, and the power responded to his will.

Once in a while, it would occur to him that New Simon was in a shit ton of trouble because addicts needed to stay away from their drugs. No more could he say he could snap his wand the moment things got too hot.

His drug was inside him. Beckoned by a split second of will.

This is what the Darkness wanted. It had him by his balls. He was on his tiptoes, one of those black threads tight around his neck. All that remained was the moment when the world fell out from under him.

Sometimes he'd tighten his grip on the steering wheel and squash the thought. Other times, the thought squashed itself. Already his power was practicing self-preservation.

Bad stuff. Magic didn't have a will of its own. By definition, it had a master. Question was: if Simon didn't master it, who did?

Only one answer to that and it was the big daddy of bad news.

Not now. Drive now. Drive and get home. Chiara first, Devil later. Just tap the tat and drive.

He glanced in the rearview mirror. No cops, no traffic, no trouble. And no nosebleed, or bloody eyes, either. He rolled his lips between his teeth. Looks like he'd banged another corner. Fantastic.

Hellfire cauterized all the bleeders, not just the ones that dripped mortal doubts.

Chiara's Place
Baltimore, MD

Simon paused on the stairs, turning to take a last look at Chiara. She lay curled up on her lousy couch, a crocheted afghan covering her from toes to chin. Only her face was visible, her eyes closed, brows drawn, a tightness around her mouth that persisted even in deep sleep. Not the most peaceful face. But it hadn't been the most peaceful of experiences, either. She was allowed to look disgruntled.

He briefly considered going outside to call Mack, try to make amends somehow. It didn't feel right, leaving things the way they did in Atlanta. He hadn't a choice, then. There was only one way to do what had to be done and he hadn't gone skipping merrily down that path, strewing daisies and singing happy songs.

He'd made a choice. Even if he wasn't entirely clear at the

time on the exact details of that choice, it was all-too clear, now. His life for hers. Since the moment she disappeared, that had been the unspoken deal.

As he gazed down at her sleeping form, her knees tucked up in a huddle, her face drawn in lines only she could interpret, he realized that, even if he'd been completely aware of the dimensions of his choice, he'd have made it all the same.

He just never anticipated that Mack would bail... but by then, it was too late. Too late. Just too fricken late.

Mack was gone.

Simon finished climbing the stairs with a softer step and quieted his mind. Least he could do is keep it down so the kid could sleep.

He glanced down the hallway, trying to remember what lay behind which doors. His bedroom was third on the left, right? Which made the spa room two doors up and opposite. Hard to remember now that he'd seen Hell's version of this place.

With a wry grin, he thought of the hot tub with it jets and bubbles. He rather liked the bubbles. Now that Chiara was home, maybe he could relax a little. Let his guard down a bit. Breathe all the way in.

Hmm. Sleep or a swim? Tough decision. Maybe a nap in the hot tub. Split the difference.

He walked down to the spa room and turned the knob. With Chiara out like a light, he wouldn't even have to swim in his briefs. Thank God. Wet underwear had a way of bunching up. No need for that special brand of hell.

He cracked the door but paused, wrinkling his nose.

Yuck. He should smell chlorine. Not...sulfur. Pushing the door open, he didn't see the hot tub.

It was the pool. The silver pool.

With a yelp, he yanked the door shut with a slam. Holy hell, how tired was he? Did he actually go all the way to the end of the hall by accident?

Looking left and right, he scratched his head. Nope. He stood right in the middle of the hall. Cautiously, he swung open the door once more, his breath catching.

The creepy pool room. Shit.

Heck, maybe he was too tired for bubbles after all. Spinning on his heel, he walked back to his bedroom. Opening the door, he saw stone tile, not plush carpeting.

Son of a bitch.

He went door to door, opening each one, save one that wouldn't budge. The silver pool. In every single room, the air was thick and curdled, smoky and sharp. Every room was the room at the end of the hall.

He rubbed his face. Probably not a glitch. That left only one thing to do.

Walking stoically to the end of the hall, he pushed open the door and stared balefully at the shimmering surface of the Devil's doorway.

"Okay. You obviously want something." He spread his hands wide. The thick air muffled his voice, swallowing any echo. "Well, here I am."

The door swung closed behind him with a boom, pushing him into the room.

"Oh. Privacy. Sure. Fine. So, talk."

Nothing.

"I got her back, didn't I?" He shook his head at the water, feeling a little self-conscious talking to a pool. "I did everything that you wanted. What more do you want?"

Only the sound of stone scraping against stone behind him. He turned, alarmed.

The wall was moving toward him.

He quickly scanned the room. All the walls were moving. Sliding. Closing in. The wall pressed against his back and pushed him forward toward the pool. He braced his shoulder and tried to push back. No use. It was solid stone and way bigger than he was. His shoes slid on the damp tiles. Closer and closer to the pool.

"Chiara!" He screamed her name until his voice cracked. "Wake up!"

He hugged the wall, going up on his toes when he slid up to the edge of the pool, bumping over the curved tiles. For a moment he hung there, precariously. Panting. Praying.

Then the wall shoved him, hard. He hit the silver surface flat on his back, and the world screamed in his ears.

Silence. And shit, the floor was hard. He'd landed on the black and white tiles with a smack that made every part of his body hurt.

It was a discomfort he quickly forgot as he looked around the room. Everything was…brighter. Like a glimmer of sunlight sparkled on every surface. The floor, the stairs, the walls— everything.

And the glimmer was magic. He felt it, a warming of the bones, as if he sunned himself on a pool-side chaise. He stared at the floor, peering intently. The glimmer came from golden lines etched into the tiles. After a moment, he saw they were letters. Words.

Familiar words.

Each tile bore a letter, forming words that repeated in a pattern he'd learned in the earliest of his studies. His lips parted in a grin.

The Devil had drawn SATOR squares all over. It was literally the oldest charm in the book.

He glanced upwards, seeing other words, other ancient charms and spells. Lucifer had His lair charmed six ways to Sunday.

And they were all protections against fire. How could he have not noticed it all before?

A familiar clearing of a throat made him turn his head.

Lucifer sat on his throne, elbows on knees, watching him with amusement. The wall behind Him looked like the lighting display at a home improvement store. The Devil had a thing for lightbulbs. "You know, you could have slipped in feet first. Makes for a better landing."

"Wasn't thinking about the best way to get here." Simon

pushed onto his elbows with a groan. "I was only thinking about how to avoid it."

"Typical human. Thinking about how you'd like to avoid going to Hell while every single thing you do drags you another step closer." Lucifer got up and paced toward Simon, panther-like and dangerous. "And another step, and another, and another, until what do you know? You're here."

Simon eyed him warily, feeling more than a few shades of vulnerable. "What do you want from me?"

Lucifer only smiled, dragon-sharp, and stretched out His hand.

To help him up.

Simon grabbed His hand—cool, not cold, not fiery, not acid-burn or electrocution. Just flesh—and pulled up to his feet, glancing around. Every lamp, every sconce was ablaze, casting shimmering false warmth onto every surface, illuminating the golden spell work. "So. Is this it? Am I a permanent fixture here?"

"No." Lucifer withdrew His hand, rubbing His fingertips against His palm. "You are not dead."

"But I'm drowning upstairs in the pool, right? Should I start running back now?"

"No. We have unfinished business." Lucifer stepped over to a side table and poured a glass of dark, red wine. "You've made excellent use of that tattoo. Am I correct in saying you've enjoyed the enhancement?"

One glass, Simon noted. The Devil was a terrible host. Not like he would have accepted a drink, but hey. Manners.

He shrugged. "It came in handy."

"Most decidedly so. You knew just what needed to be done and had no regard for the cost."

An over-reaching statement. The costs had simply been too numerous to tally. He remembered every nosebleed, every wave of pain, every conviction that he was bleeding to death from the inside. The symptoms had stopped in Atlanta—especially the bloody eyes, praise Jesus—but he hadn't considered himself cured. More like a new stage of terminal. "Not like I enjoyed it."

"Who would? Not you. You send demons back to Hell. Exorcists don't wield hell fire. But you did, didn't you? You tapped into a power you never imagined possible. And it was killing you, wasn't it?" He paused for a long swallow of wine, His eyes alight with a silver gleam, before setting down the glass on the mantelpiece. "Did it stop you? Of course not. Not Simon Alliant. The unstoppable exorcist, kicking all my messengers back home, one by one by one. The hell fire erupted in your hands and you exorcised by the dozens. Incredible!"

Simon stared at the floor, the light from a thousand lamps puddling at his feet. Thin shadows flickered at the edges, held back by the flood of light. He titled his head, eyes shifting. A memory of something he'd read. A memory that was only now triggered. It itched in his brain like a cadaver worm, digging its way to the surface.

Lucifer clapped His hands together, each slap measured and hollow. "Even I was impressed. Even more so when you destroyed an angel."

The Devil smiled and wagged a finger at him in admiration. "But you—you laughed in the face of sense and self-preservation. And conventional wisdom, too. Hell gates are not supposed to exist. Yet, you know they do. You saw your first one, in Baltimore, months ago. Then you opened one, just for me."

Simon felt like a traitorous wretch. Hanging was too good for him. Every unspoken vow he'd ever made had been broken in that moment, when he did the worst thing he could imagine. He did open a hell gate. He did give Lucifer access to their plane, even if only for a few moments. What he'd done wasn't just sinful. It was abominable.

And it had saved Chiara. That was the only thing that kept his pieces together. She was worth it. She was worth everything.

"I must say." Lucifer's voice took on a curious tone, one that raised the hair on Simon's neck. Clasping His hands behind

His back, the Devil slowly paced a slow circle around him, momentarily blocking each lamp as He passed in front. "It was a bracing feeling, watching you open that gate. A door opened, right here, right where you stand now. I didn't even have to go looking for it."

Simon wiped his mouth, watching Lucifer's deliberate circuit, the play of shadow passing in front of the light. Where the hell was He going with all this?

"And although you and I accomplished a significant task, I am left feeling…disquiet. Not because I have the misfortune of listening to Luminea's endless complaints." Lucifer dragged His fingertips through the hair at His temple, sounding harried. "Really, she hates me. It's going to be a long time before she slows her tirade."

"She's a little bit of a bitch," Simon admitted.

Lucifer chuckled and nodded. "A little bit, yes. But she has earned the right. I did a terrible thing to her. I hadn't realized how she had rotted away inside. The only thing worse than a righteous hate is a love that has eroded into pain. A love ripped away, leaving one stranded in darkness. That transcends hate. And you…"

Simon swallowed hard, his throat bobbing painfully. "Me?"

"I just plain-old ordinary hate you." Lucifer shook His head slightly, wearing a bemused expression. "So, no big thing. And, no hard feelings, really. It was a mutually beneficial partnership. But I do not like how comfortable you've become wearing my mark. It made you bolder than you should have been."

Simon rubbed his shoulder, where Lucifer's hand print stained him. "This? I hadn't even known it was there until—"

"Not that mark. The other." Lucifer pointed a finger at Simon's arm and swirled His fingertip in a circle.

The tattoo lit up, a pulse of light that zipped around the outer edge, a searing sting chasing behind. Pain and power exploded behind Simon's eyes and he spasmed, every muscle locking. Doubling over, he cried out, convulsing, sucking breath.

Lucifer leaned over him. "My mark and the power that came with it. The hell fire. The height and the expanse of limitless power. Every time you tapped into it, it just got better. Stronger. Higher. You knew it. And you knew that it would kill you if you kept using it. Trouble is…"

The Devil crossed His arms. "You didn't die. Not even when that petty Watcher withdrew his support. You should have died opening that hell gate. That was the plan. So, now I must come up with a new plan. I don't like knowing that the very first hell gate you opened was right here, to this very spot, inside my fortress. I don't like knowing you can survive after using my power. You've proved you can tap into my eminence any time you choose, take what you need, and do what you like with it. And I don't like sharing."

The pain was receding, allowing him to choke out words between gasps. He slowly straightened. "I..imagine that's…how you…would feel."

"Yes, well, try to imagine what it will feel like when I take it away."

He rolled his widened eyes up at the King of Hell, panicking. "Wait—what?"

With a gesture of curling fingers, Lucifer beckoned to the remnant of power that had been residing in Simon. The tattoo glowed once more, brighter than the lanterns that lined the room, and emitted a searing pain as it lifted itself from his skin. The power, a streak of mercury, writhed up into the air, away from Simon.

He roared with agony. His arm was being ripped apart, like a giant claw just hooked into his tattoo and tore it away. Pain so massive he saw it, saw the color of pain because he could see nothing else. An Enochian nut-crushing had nothing on this.

So. This is what Hell feels like.

After what felt like an eternity, the pain began to abate. His vision slowly cleared, but remained dim. The glimmer of Lucifer's protection spells had vanished. Stripped of the tattoo, his link to the Devil, Simon realized he'd lost the ability to read

His spell work.

He felt…denied. It was a terrible thing to feel. No exorcist should miss being one with the King of Hell.

Through the bleary haze, Simon looked up at Lucifer's smile.

The Devil's face was illuminated by the glow of His many lamps, only His eyes holding the shadows. The shadows and the silver gleam of the Morningstar, the Light that Fell into Darkness.

And here he was, on his knees before the Devil again. This was getting to be a habit.

"That's better. " Lucifer tugged His sleeves straight. "Good to have all of me back again."

Simon held his arm, tears stinging his eyes. It still hurt like shit. And suddenly, more than anything, he needed a smoke.

Lucifer walked over to the mantle, reaching for His wine glass. "Feeling more like your old self, magician?"

More and more, he thought, *and not all of it helpful.* Funny how much his old self was full of the wrong stuff. At least his sense of sarcasm hadn't been altered by the experience. Simon raised his left hand toward the Devil's back, giving him the finger.

"I saw that," Lucifer said. "Oh, by the way?"

He pointed overhead and smirked over His shoulder. "Now. Now, you should run."

Simon felt the burn in his chest before he could even get to his feet. Leveling a glare at Lucifer, wearing a smile that said *oh, you son of a whore,* he banged it up the steps and raced for the hazel pool. Laughter was a phantom rider on his heels.

Running from the Devil, again. Another habit.

Finally, a habit he hoped never to break.

The story will continue in
THE ABSENT-MINDED MAGICIAN
(The Demon Whisperer #3)

ABOUT THE AUTHOR

USA Today best-selling author **Ash Krafton** is a speculative fiction author from the Pennsylvania coal region. If she's not writing, it's probably because she's distracted by all the cool junk on her desk or by the stacks of books that have grown up around it.

She writes novels, short fiction, and poetry for mostly adult audiences. (She's *mostly* an adult.). Some of those novels are:

The Books of the Demimonde
(urban fantasy trilogy)

Enter the world of the Demimonde.

Look outside your window. Same old town, same streets, same people, same stories you've lived all your life. Or... are they?

Sophie Galen is an advice columnist from the suburbs of Philly. Like many sensitive women, she's done her best to create a shelter for herself in order to live in a safe, predictable world, protecting her vulnerable self: her mind, her heart, her soul.

Then he came into her life and blew the walls in.

When Marek Thurzo arrived, he brought with him all the secrets she never wanted to know: the world outside was not what she thought. There were people and creatures and powers she'd never dared to believe exist and at the very center of this humongous supernatural web was one single person.

Her. The Sophia. The one hope for redemption for the Demivampire race.

Some days, she still can't wrap her head around the whole thing. Other days...

...she's ready to do whatever it takes to protect her demivamps, no matter the obstacle, no matter the enemy, no matter the personal

cost.

While meeting her deadlines, of course. Who says a girl can't multitask while saving the world?

Bleeding Hearts (Demimonde #1)
Blood Rush (Demimonde #2)
Wolf's Bane (Demimonde #3)

Available in ebook and paperback
Audiobook versions in production

WORDS THAT BIND
(paranormal romance)

Social worker Tam Kerish can't keep her cool professionalism when steamy client Mr. Burns kindles a desire for more than a client-therapist relationship—so she drops him. However, they discover she's the talisman to which Burns, an immortal djinn, has been bound since the days of King Solomon…and that makes it difficult to stay away from him.

Ethical guidelines are unequivocal when it comes to personal relationships with clients. However, the djinn has a thawing effect on the usually non-emotive Tam, who begins to feel true emotion whenever he is near. Tam has to make a difficult choice: to stay on the outside, forever looking in…or to turn her back on her entire world, just for the chance to finally experience what it means to fall in love.

Ash also writes New Adult spec fic as AJ Krafton. **THE HEARTBEAT THIEF** (Victorian fantasy) is a little bit Jane Austen, a little bit Edgar Allan Poe, and a whole lot of stealing heartbeats in order to stay young and beautiful forever... How far will Senza Fyne go to avoid Death?

"There was something smart, ominous, and romantic about this strange story..."

The Heartbeat Thief by AJ Krafton

Join the Fictitious Initiative...

If you'd like an email whenever Ash (or AJ) has a new release, great giveaway, or special offer, you can sign up at http://www.subscribepage.com/b1w9p1. Your email will never be shared and you can unsubscribe at any time.

Thanks for reading!

Word-of-mouth is crucial for any author to succeed. If you've enjoyed reading this book, please consider leaving a brief review—just a line or two is fine, and it may help another reader decide to give this book a try. And if you *really* enjoyed reading it, tell a friend. Friends share :)